Hideaway
in
Iceland

Victoria Walker

ISBN: 978-1-7399441-2-4

For Jake

x

1

Anna Mortimer stood outside the church and leant back on the Cotswold stone wall that had been warmed by the late summer sun. She'd done it. She'd pulled off the deal of a lifetime and it felt amazing.

The biggest exclusive deal that had ever been done with a glossy celebrity magazine for the wedding of the year, maybe of the decade, had gone without a hitch. Not one single paparazzi photographer had been lurking in the bushes or behind a gravestone and a very happy Mr and Mrs Banks were about to emerge from the picturesque little church.

Anna moved her sunglasses down from the top of her head and headed for the lychgate, the arched stone entrance to the churchyard, beyond which the cars were waiting. Once the happy couple were safely away in the bridal car — less bridal and more huge black car with blacked-out windows — she could get back to London with a feather in her cap and hopefully a huge number of new clients who would want her to do the same for them.

Ever since boyband member Freddie Banks and UK actress-turned-Hollywood star Sophia Hamilton had started their relationship two years ago, there had been a media frenzy surrounding them wherever they went. Never mind that Freddie was less baby-faced poster boy now that he was on the wrong side of thirty, his band The Rush were still hitting the number one spot with everything they released. This was despite the fact that Ned Nokes, arguably the most popular member — there was always talk of rivalry between him and Freddie — had recently left the band. Freddie's people had asked Anna's firm to negotiate an exclusive deal for them for the wedding coverage in the hope of being able to control the media and make an attempt at having a private wedding. She'd been the conduit between the Hey! team, the wedding planner and the lawyers.

There was movement from the door of the church and a handful of black-suited security guards exited first, checking that the coast was clear before Freddie and Sophia walked, beaming at each other, out into the sunshine of the idyllic Cotswold churchyard.

Anna watched from the gate, smiling at what looked like any couple in love on their wedding day, glad that she was able to contribute to making that happen for them. Their guests followed them outside, wandering along the grassy pathways that meandered between the ancient higgledy-piggledy gravestones. The team from Hey! magazine were taking informal shots of the guests, hoping to capture the palpable joy of the occasion. Amongst the crowd were just a handful of people Anna didn't recognise, presumably the happy couple's family. Most of the guests were A-list celebrities and, Anna noticed, even Ned Nokes had turned up despite speculation that now he'd left the band he and Freddie would no longer need to pretend to get along. It was heartening to see that they were friends, whatever the press said, as Anna watched Ned congratulate Freddie with a bear hug and a ruffle of his immaculate hair which Freddie laughed off before good-naturedly returning the gesture.

Ned was looking fantastic actually, in the smart navy-blue

suit which showed off his slim figure and long limbs to perfection. It was a million miles away from his usual outfit of jeans and a scruffy — but probably expensive — t-shirt and scuffed black Doc Marten boots. Anna had never seen him close-up before and was surprised that he wasn't as tall as she'd thought, definitely shy of six feet but his trademark quiff, that he was now re-perfecting by raking it through with his fingers, probably added a couple of inches.

Just as everyone began to head to their cars, there was an intense buzzing noise. Quiet at first but quickly becoming louder as it came into sight over the roof of the church, hovering over the heads of the crowd. It was a drone.

Anna's heart immediately began palpitating. This was the worst thing that could have happened and at the worst possible moment. In the few seconds since it had been hovering, it would already have footage of every guest at the wedding and whoever owned the drone would have the pictures online before you could even begin to do anything about it.

Sophia squealed, covered her head with her bouquet and ran back into the church, closely followed by Freddie and then all of the other guests. The bemused family members were bringing up the rear at a decidedly less frantic pace. Although Anna had no idea what she could suggest as a plan of action, her gut feeling was that it probably would have been better to get the whole thing over and done with by getting everyone away in the cars because now they were all being held hostage in the church by a drone.

Quickly coming to terms with the fact that as the man on the ground, as it were, she was going to have to help rectify the situation, Anna gathered herself, smoothed down the skirt of her black 1950s-style dress, raised her sunglasses back onto the top of her head and made her way towards the church. She stood in the porch where the door was ajar and took a moment to plan what she might say before facing the wrath of the Hey! team and the wedding planner.

Just as she took a deep breath and reached to pull the door open, it opened towards her, and she stumbled backwards to avoid being hit by it.

'Oh…!' As she felt herself about to lose her footing completely, a firm hand grabbed her forearm and she managed to steady herself.

'I'm sorry. Are you okay?'

She looked up to find Ned Nokes himself stood right in front of her, so close that as she righted herself, she was looking straight at his designer stubble and thinking, bizarrely, that if she took a deep breath, their chests would probably touch. His hand was still on her arm, and she was so caught up in the moment that she couldn't move. She risked a breath and leant back slightly, just in case her right breast grazed his chest. Oh, he smelt amazing. Expensive and clean and… gorgeous.

Her eyes raised to meet his.

'Thank you, I'm fine.'

The concern in his eyes disappeared and was replaced by relief as he smiled.

'Good.' He let her arm go but stayed where he was.

For a few minutes — realistically it was seconds, Anna knew when she replayed it in her mind later — they looked at each other, her blue eyes meeting his brown ones. Something was happening but inevitably the moment was broken by the persistent buzzing of the drone.

'You should go inside until it's clear,' Anna suggested, suddenly remembering her reason for being there.

He shrugged. 'Think they've probably got what they came for and it's not me, anyway.'

'Um, I would beg to differ,' Anna said with a small snort of laughter which she instantly regretted. If there was ever a time to be composed and alluring, it was now. 'I think you're probably at the top of their list since you left the band. Everyone wants to know what you've been up to.' She blushed at her frankness. She was unable to temper herself most of the time, but she usually tried to be more tactful around clients and celebrities. Why was that deserting her when she was having a conversation with one of the most famous people in the world?

'Nothing exciting, to be honest,' he said.

She wasn't asking him, didn't he realise that?

'Right. Well, I don't think they care what you're actually doing, they just want pictures of you doing something. I think they'll be quite pleased with this.' She waved her hand between them.

'You think they'll assume I came to the wedding with you?'

'Oh god. I hope not. No offence.'

'None taken,' he said with raised eyebrows and a grin. 'Are you going to make a run for it then?'

He seemed to have forgotten that she was trying to get into the church, although she'd almost forgotten that too.

'Not yet. I think the battery on that will be dead in another couple of minutes,' she said, peering out of the porch and pointing to the drone, 'and then everyone can leave before it comes back.'

'Good plan. Perhaps we should get everyone ready to go?'

With Ned at the door ready to give the signal when the drone had gone, Anna stood at the front of the church and announced that everyone should be ready to head for the cars at lightning speed once he gave the signal.

'Now!' shouted Ned, flinging both doors open to allow the stream of guests outside quickly. By the time Anna brought up the rear, Freddie, Sophia and Ned had all disappeared along with the other A-listers, leaving just the bemused family members and an angry-looking photography crew behind.

'Literally the worst timing for you to have a leak in your team,' said the photography assistant while they waited for his boss to get off the phone with hers.

'It wasn't our team, Daniel.'

Anna had known him for a few years. He turned up on lots of shoots and revelled in any drama that might come up.

'You might have a hard time proving that. They'd sent out all the invitations with a different church and reception venue and only told the guests once they'd arrived there. It was like a military operation, you know that.'

'Well, the deal is the biggest our agency has ever done, we're hardly likely to jeopardise that, are we?'

He shrugged. 'I don't know what your motives are, but it'll be the end of Lime PR.'

Well, that wasn't true. She gave him a hard stare to leave him in no doubt that she thought he was talking nonsense and he wandered off to chat to the wedding planner's assistant instead.

Anna knew it wasn't her who had leaked the details but unfortunately, she knew that Daniel was probably right. No one had known the actual venue other than two colleagues at Lime PR, the wedding planner, Hey! magazine and Freddie and Sophia. Even the reception venue hadn't been told who their newlyweds were, and Anna couldn't for the life of her think what any of those people had to gain by leaking anything.

'Right, we're going ahead to the reception venue,' the photographer announced to his team. 'We'll salvage what we can. Apparently, more celebrities are turning up there who weren't at the church so we might get something even if the pictures from here get out before ours.'

'Great,' said Anna, relieved that they weren't abandoning it altogether. 'And how good can those drone pictures be anyway?'

The Hey! team all stared at her as if she'd just announced that she was the leak after all.

'I think we all know they'll be good enough,' the photographer said with a grimace.

The drive back to London seemed to take forever. Anna was flipping between puzzling over the mystery of who had leaked the details and the surreal moment when she'd met Ned Nokes in the church porch. Both things were unsettling and unexpected and had thrown Anna out of her usual comfort zone of being in control of just about everything in her life.

If she'd met Ned Nokes in any other situation, if he'd been an ordinary bloke in a bar, it would have hit her like a thunderbolt. Wouldn't it? That had never happened to her. It astounded her to hear about people finding The One or to hear about people who said it was like electricity when they first touched the love of their life. None of those things were true, she was pretty sure. Until today. There was something there, definitely, but then she had been feeling extremely stressed out. Perhaps that had contributed to the feelings that she'd had in those few minutes. Something to do with adrenaline? Perhaps normally, if her heart hadn't already been beating ten to the dozen, she would have met him and felt nothing. But she didn't believe that. And it didn't matter anyway. He was Ned Nokes and she'd probably never see him again.

2

Before either of them had said a word, Giles slammed copies of several tabloid newspapers onto his desk, one at a time. Anna had already seen them, he'd know she had, but he loved a bit of theatre.

'And all before the Hey! exclusive has even gone to print, let alone made it to the shelves,' he said as he threw the final copy onto the desk with a flourish.

The photos from the drone were grainy but still front-page worthy. You could clearly make out Sophia's dress in a shot of her fleeing back into the church and there was a shot of her and Freddie kissing outside the church, probably in the moment just before they realised what was happening.

'It's awful, I know but I don't think there was anything we could have done differently.'

'Short of us suggesting that they hold the ceremony after dark to avoid the bloody drones getting a decent shot, I would agree,' he said with a grimace. 'Nevertheless, Anna, we have to be able to assure clients that even if they're the most famous couple in the world, it's within our abilities to help them get married in the middle of the day like every other couple in the world without ruining their ability to cash in on that.'

'I know that Giles, but I honestly did everything I could to mitigate the situation once we realised what was happening.'

'Are you telling me that it wasn't you that leaked it?'

'Of course it wasn't me!' She was incredulous that he could even think that. They'd worked together for ten years and until now she thought he knew that her integrity was everything to her. 'I've been wracking my brains since Saturday, and I just don't know what happened.'

'Unfortunately, we can't be seen to sweep this under the carpet. If we ever want to deal with Hey! magazine again we need to identify the leak and deal with it. Publicly.'

'So, what do you suggest? An investigation? There was only you, me and Polly who knew the actual details.'

'And you're sure there's no way that anyone else in the office could have had access?'

'Absolutely not, at least not from me.'

'I'm going to assume that you're not insinuating it was me and I think we can both agree that it wouldn't have been Polly.'

Anna reluctantly had to agree. Polly was in her sixties and had been with the agency longer than Giles. She'd gone from starting out as the switchboard operator to being his PA and was the most trusted person in the agency, possibly in the PR world as a whole, because of her reputation for discretion. It wasn't Polly.

'Unless you can offer me any other viable explanation, I'm afraid I'm going to have to let you go.'

Anna was stunned. Did she hear that right? He was going to fire her?

'But it wasn't me, Giles.'

'Can you prove that?'

'Can't you take my word for it?'

'Anna, I believe you, but I need to tackle this. Today. We have to redeem our reputation as quickly as possible. You understand.'

'I do… but it'll ruin my career. And Hey! will still sell just as many copies because people will want the story, not just these crap grainy pictures.' Her voice was full of desperation now that she knew this conversation was the only thing between her and unemployment.

Giles looked uncomfortable for the first time since the conversation started.

'It'll blow over. Take a couple of weeks' downtime, something will come up.'

Her career wouldn't repair itself in the space of a couple of weeks. She could understand Giles's problem, but she didn't want to be the solution.

'Can you give me some time to look into it? See if I can find out what happened. I could ring a couple of my contacts at these papers and see if they'll give me a name.'

'They'll protect their sources, you know that. Especially sources that have been so lucrative for them. I'm sorry, Anna. I do have to let you go.'

Now she realised why Giles had called the meeting so early in the morning. It was so that she could quietly leave the building with some of her dignity intact before her colleagues arrived for work. She packed up her desk, fighting back tears even though there was no one there to see but if she allowed herself to cry now, she might not be able to stop. She wasn't about to take the Tube home carrying a cardboard box with a tear-stained face because then everyone would know.

The cardboard box of shame was hidden away in the spare room and Anna was waiting for the kettle to boil. She had no idea what to do. Her head felt like it was full of fluff, and she couldn't think straight. The kettle was taking too long, and would a cup of tea really help in a situation like this anyway? Instead, she pulled out a bottle of tequila from the cupboard and poured herself a shot.

She held the small shot glass with her fingertips, wondering whether this was the beginning of a slippery slope into daytime drinking but reminding herself that her career had just crumbled to nothing in the space of a couple of hours. She downed the shot and poured another. Desperate times. Oddly, the warmth of the tequila spreading down her throat seemed to help, and she did then make a cup of tea and took it into the lounge.

Since the drone incident on Saturday, she hadn't dared look at any press or social media. When she'd got to work that morning she'd taken ten minutes to look at as much as she could before the meeting with Giles. Until then she'd seen no papers or news websites and no terrestrial television. She had very successfully buried her head in the sand. On some level, she'd known that something like this could happen, but she didn't seriously think she'd be out of a job because of it. Should she try and find out what happened? It hardly seemed worth it now. It wasn't as if Giles would welcome her back with open arms if she could blame it on someone else and anyway, she had some dignity. Now that she'd finished traipsing the streets and the Tube with a cardboard box filled with a Ficus plant that she'd had trouble seeing past, now she had dignity.

Emboldened by the tequila, Anna thought it was worth calling a couple of friends in other PR agencies, just to see how the land lay. Did anyone even know what had happened? How fast did word about things like this really spread?

'Hi, Abbie, how's it going?'

'Christ, Anna, what are you calling here for?' Her friend was loud-whispering down the phone as if people could see them physically talking to each other.

'I just wondered whether you'd heard about the wedding.'

'Have I heard? Everybody's heard. I can't believe you rocked up this morning as if nothing had happened. You blew the biggest contract in history.'

Tears sprang into Anna's eyes as she heard the brutal truth about how people, colleagues who until now she would have counted as friends, thought it had played out. It hadn't taken long for word to spread that it was apparently down to her leaking the details.

'Well, um... thanks, Abbie. If anything comes up — 'Why did she say that? Because she already knew what the answer would be.

'I won't be calling and if you have any sense, don't call anywhere else either. Bye.'

It hurt. More than anything that had happened to her before. It made her ache and crying seemed to be the only thing to do to make it stop. She hugged herself and sobbed at the loss of her career and, if she was honest, her life. She had nothing. Without her job, she had no friends and no life. It was so unfair that when she'd literally given over her life to her career at the cost of... well, lots of things, it could all end over something that wasn't even her fault.

It might have seemed melodramatic to think that she had nothing, but it was the truth. Since her best friend, Rachel, had moved to Iceland five months ago to be with the love of her life, Jonas, Anna had realised that all her other friends were actually just work contacts. All her socialising was work-related, and she had no one to call if she just wanted to go to the cinema or out for a drink. She was an idiot not to have seen it before. She'd turned into a workaholic without even noticing, she'd thought she was riding high on success, measured by more invitations than she had time to accept.

Rachel used to love tagging along in the hope of coming across a celebrity or two and she missed that. It always gave her a bit of perspective, reminding her that she was lucky to be doing what she was doing. Lucky that it didn't feel like a job most of the time. Perhaps Rachel could give her the perspective she needed now. Maybe she could see a way forward that Anna hadn't thought of. At the very least she'd be a sympathetic ear.

'Hi, Rach, how are you?'

'I can't believe you've made me wait two days for the low-down on Freddie's wedding! I don't know how I've held back from ringing you, but I knew you'd be busy. Was it amazing?'

Anna waited for Rachel to get her pent-up excitement out. She couldn't have got a word in edgeways anyway.

'I think I even saw a picture of you online somewhere. Outside the church would it have been? Jonas was sure it was you, even though you've not met yet, he's seen you on enough FaceTime calls to know.'

'Mmm, it might have been me.' She'd seen a grainy picture of her and Ned Nokes peering out of the church porch, but it was so enlarged that it was hard to tell who it was really unless someone told you.

'Well, I knew it was you because you were wearing that 50s dress that you look amazing in.'

'Thanks, Rach.'

'So… you sound a bit down.'

And that was why she'd called Rachel. They knew each other so well that some things didn't need explaining.

'I've lost my job.'

'Anna, no! Why?'

'Someone leaked the location of the wedding and a drone swept in and scuppered the exclusive. You shouldn't have seen any photos anywhere yet. That's the problem.'

'But it wasn't you.'

'No, but I can't prove how it happened, so it comes down to me. There's no one else they can blame.'

'That's so unfair.'

It felt unfair and Anna had another cry and a rant to her friend about the injustice of it all and what the hell was she going to do now that she was ostracised from the only industry she'd ever known.

'Come to Iceland.'

'I don't know, Rach. It feels like the wrong time to be going off on holiday. I need to find a job.'

'You can't get a job at the moment, you said that yourself. Look, if you sort your airfare you can stay with me and Jonas. It'll be a bit tight, but we'd love to have you. And it's brilliant timing because I could do with a hand on the marketing side of my new business.'

Anna perked up. It'd be like a working holiday, and she'd get to see her friend, see the place and the man she'd fallen in love with.

'I'd love something like that to get stuck into, actually Rach. It'd be a great distraction.'

'And you want to see me and meet Jonas in real life.'

'Obviously.' Anna smiled, suddenly feeling like a weight had lifted off her now that she had a plan for at least the next few weeks. 'I did meet Ned Nokes.'

'Oh my god! I can't believe you didn't tell me that straight away! Did you get a picture with him?'

Never let a friend's misery get in the way of a celebrity story. Typical Rachel. But it made Anna smile again.

'No, I was busy stressing about what to do about the drone. But he was nice.'

'Nice?'

'He smelt nice, and he was chatty.' And now she regretted telling Rachel because Ned Nokes was something more to her than just a celebrity she met. That moment they'd shared in the porch was hers and she wished she had kept it to herself.

3

Sophia was cooking, something Ned had never witnessed before in all the time he'd spent sitting at the enormous kitchen island in Freddie's basement in Kensington. He raised an eyebrow at Freddie, inclining his head towards Sophia as she cracked another egg into a frying pan.

'What can I say? She loves cooking for her husband,' Freddie said with a grin.

'I'm cooking enough for you too, Ned.'

'What is it?' Sophia didn't strike him as a cook. He'd never seen her in the kitchen except to fetch a bottle of Prosecco from the fridge.

'Huevos Rancheros,' she said confidently.

'We had it every morning on our honeymoon,' Freddie explained. 'We're addicted and Soph has been trying to replicate it every morning since we got back.'

'Trying?'

Freddie put a finger to his lips and frowned at Ned. 'It's amazing, mate. Wait 'til you try it.'

It was a pretty nice breakfast. Better than the couple of slices of toast that would have been the only option at his own house. It had been a tough few weeks and shopping for anything but the basics had gone out of the window.

'Thanks, Sophia, that was really tasty. I loved the smashed tomatoes, that was a nice twist.'

'Aw, thanks Ned'

Freddie got up from his stool and looped his arms around her waist. 'Okay if me and Ned shoot?'

'Of course, baby.'

Some kissing and other behaviour only associated with newlyweds ensued, so Ned headed for the stairs to give them some privacy.

It was strange seeing Freddie married. Somehow it changed things between them and that made Ned even more certain that it had been the right time to leave the band. Out of the four of them, he and Freddie had always been best friends. They were all mates, but they had naturally gravitated towards spending more time together and the same was true for Joe and Alex. Now he'd left them as a trio, he wasn't sure how it would work. But Freddie having Sophia helped to ease any guilt he might have felt about it.

'Sorry about that,' said Freddie bounding up the stairs. 'Studio?'

'Yeah.'

They headed up to the top floor where Freddie's studio cum man-cave was located. It wasn't set up for proper recording, but it was sound-proofed, and they used it for writing because it had the right vibe. But today they were just catching up with each other after Freddie's couple of weeks away on a super-yacht in the Caribbean. When Ned was struggling with the idea of quitting the band, this had been where those difficult conversations had taken place with Freddie, Joe and Alex and now he needed a bit of reassurance from his friend, it was the right place to be.

'How's it been?' Freddie asked as he settled himself into a furry beanbag and snapped the top off a bottle of water.

'It's weird. I knew it would be but it's like I had this big plan when I left the band and now, I don't know what to do next.'

'Have you been writing?'

'Not really. I can't get down to it.'

He paused, unsure whether unburdening himself to his friend was the right call. He'd just come back from his honeymoon, for god's sake.

But Freddie was waiting for Ned to speak, knowing that something was coming.

'I'm worried I might have made a mistake leaving the band.' Just saying it out loud made him feel lighter.

Freddie pushed himself up and poured some whisky into a pair of heavy cut-glass tumblers. He passed one to Ned who was lying on his side on a sheepskin rug on the floor.

'Thanks, mate.'

'Look, I know it must feel strange. It was a big decision, but it was the right one, Ned. You've always planned this, always been honest with us that the band wasn't your dream.'

'What do I do now? Am I supposed to just relaunch myself, go through the whole machine again from the start?'

'Yes, but the difference is this time it's what you want. You're not being manipulated or manufactured. This time it can be on your terms. That's the point.

'I don't know if I thought it through properly. I mean, I don't have a label or a manager or anything.'

'Ned, get a fucking grip. You're one of the richest people in the country. This isn't starting from nowhere. It's being in an amazing position that allows you to follow your dream.'

'But the whole world is watching and waiting for me to fail.'

'I didn't see you in the drone photos, mate, and you were the only one out there once we'd made a run for it.'

'Not true,' Ned said, holding his glass towards Freddie to

emphasise his point. 'There was an article on some website that said that wedding planner woman was my date for the wedding. They had a photo of us.' He laughed. 'But I take your point.'

He thought back to that moment in the church porch with the woman who looked chic, even when she'd snorted with derision at him. He smiled as he remembered. She stood out from the crowd of women who usually surrounded him and perhaps that was why.

'That wedding planner, the one who made the announcement about the drone. Have you met her before?'

Freddie shrugged. 'I don't think so. Maybe Soph has. Want me to ask?'

'No, don't worry,' he said automatically, immediately feeling disappointed, 'but she said that everyone's waiting to see what I do next.'

'That was quite a conversation with a stranger in a couple of minutes,' he joked before adopting a more serious tone. 'Can it be anything like the scrutiny we've had over the past ten years? I mean, think about what it was like in the beginning. When we were like, twenty and the fans were everywhere, all the time?'

'Thank god it's not like that anymore.'

'And, no offence mate, but I doubt it'll be like that again. Your wedding planner woman just meant the press, I expect, and we'll always have to deal with them whatever we're doing.'

'I guess so. I know leaving the band doesn't switch all that stuff off. I just feel like I need time to sort myself out.'

'Just do what you want to do. Leaving was the hard part.'

Ned drank the rest of the whisky and laid back on the rug, running his fingers through his hair.

'Shit, you're right, Fred. I have nothing riding on this. No one's watching me, who fucking cares, right?'

'Right. Do your thing, Neddy boy. Live like no one's watching.'

After a couple of hours and a few more drinks, Ned headed home, his beanie hat pulled low despite the warmth of the weather and despite there being no sign of any paparazzi when he left Freddie's. A plan was beginning to form in his head. For the first time since he'd left the band, he was starting to sense the beginnings of a way forward and it put a spring in his step.

His own place was a short walk from Freddie's. It was a smaller, terraced townhouse which was spacious and light inside but felt safe and comfortable. A real bolthole with a walled garden just big enough to give him the privacy he wanted. The long terraced row of white Georgian houses meant that he could spot a pap a mile off.

He let himself in and headed into the kitchen, opening the bi-fold doors to let the warmth of the day in. He poured a glass of water to try and dilute the effects of the whisky and opened his laptop on the breakfast bar. He needed to take some time to mull things over, maybe start writing. Going somewhere else might be a good idea. Somewhere with no distractions where he could gather his thoughts and get a feel for what he was going to do.

In the past ten years that he'd been in the band, he'd contributed to writing their songs but had been quietly working on his own as well. He'd discovered a natural country-slash-folky vibe in himself that was so far removed from the pop classics The Rush produced, that he'd never have been able to release a solo single while he was still part of that. So, he'd gradually built up a stash of songs that he was proud of. They needed work and they needed to work together if he was going to think about releasing them but now that he could just get on and do that, he realised that this next step needed careful curation.

With Google open, the curser flashing at him, inviting him to search for the perfect place to go, he was at a loss. He'd been almost everywhere with the lads. There wasn't anywhere that stood out enough for it to be the obvious choice for his music writing retreat, as he'd started to think of it. He eventually typed, 'city retreat Airbnb not UK.' A hotel wasn't really an option for what he wanted.

He clicked on the top result and found himself looking at a penthouse apartment overlooking the harbour in Reykjavik, Iceland. Being somewhere he'd miraculously never been to, it piqued his interest and he clicked again to find out more. It took him down a rabbit hole into a couple of hours of solid research on Reykjavik and he felt such an affinity with the idea, that he booked the place for three months.

Reykjavik seemed perfect. A city, and yet it was small. Only a three-hour flight and the most amazing apartment for a fraction of the cost of somewhere similar in London. The view of the harbour and the mountains across the bay were what appealed to him, knowing that writing was a lonely business and that feeling connected was something he would crave.

Once he'd booked a flight that left the day after tomorrow, he closed his laptop and pulled a beer out of the fridge, taking it into the garden to sip on while he messaged his friends and family to tell them his plans.

His finger hovered over Jeannie's name. It was nothing serious. He didn't need to tell her, she'd find out anyway once The Rush's people found out from Freddie and the lads. But he wasn't that guy that could call on someone for a hook-up now and again without it meaning anything, so he sent her a brief message to say that he'd be out of town for a while. That was enough.

4

Wasn't it still supposed to be summer? It had looked like summer from the plane window, with the endless blue skies, calm seas and no snow in sight, but most of the people getting off the plane were pulling on coats and hats as if it were the depths of winter. Rachel had said to bring a coat, but it was September, so Anna had packed it in her hold luggage. Anyway, perhaps these people just didn't have room for their coats in their bags so were wearing them for ease.

It had been a tough couple of weeks and the thought of coming to Iceland had been a welcome light at the end of a tunnel of self-doubt and feelings of worthlessness that had enveloped her since she'd been fired. If she'd not had the trip to plan, she knew that by now she'd have sunken into a dark place that might have been hard to emerge from. Even the few days she'd had between deciding to come and getting on the flight had made her realise that her life had been superficial. What did she have that actually mattered, once her career that touched every aspect of her life with its glitter was swept away? Coming to terms with that was hard and she was struggling with feelings that sometimes engulfed her; that she had wasted her life, had no meaningful relationships other than with Rachel and her family and had nothing to show for any of it apart from a wardrobe of clothes and shoes that she might never need to wear again.

Rachel had said she'd be there to meet her, but Anna was taken aback to find her and Jonas waiting in the arrival's hall at Keflavik airport with a huge banner that said, 'Welcome to Iceland, Anna!'

She dropped her case in front of them, laughing out loud at the ridiculous yet touching sign and threw her arms around Rachel.

'I love the sign!'

'I'm so glad you're here!'

They stopped hugging but stood looking at each other, holding hands still, grinning like lunatics while Jonas moved in to pick up Anna's case.

'Oh, Jonas this is Anna,' Rachel said, stating the obvious.

'Nice to meet you, Anna,' he said, leaning in to kiss her on the cheek and hugging her with his free arm at the same time.

'Nice to meet you. You're more handsome in real life.'

He blushed and smiled while Rachel laughed. 'See?' she said.

'I do see,' Anna said, linking arms with her friend as they followed Jonas out of the terminal building. If she'd been shocked that her friend had made a life-changing move to Iceland in March, now she could already see the easy chemistry between Rachel and Jonas, she understood. It was something she'd never seen between Rachel and her ex, Adam, and both of them looked so happy.

'Christ, it's freezing!' Although it looked warm, there was a cold wind and Anna immediately understood why everyone on the plane was wearing a coat.

'The car is just over here,' said Jonas, pointing.

Anna realised that she'd seriously misunderstood the concept of an Icelandic September. She had packed way too lightly. Even her coat might not be up to the job of keeping her warm.

'Is it always this cold?'

'No, this is quite warm for September,' said Jonas, who looked like he was dressed to hike up a mountain.

'You'll get used to it,' Rachel said, hugging Anna's arm affectionately. 'I hardly notice it anymore and at least you've come before the snow arrives again.'

'Mmm.'

'You will love it.' Jonas grinned at her as they reached the jeep, and he stowed her case in the back. 'Rachel has so many things to show you.'

Rachel insisted on sitting in the back seat with Anna while Jonas did the driving.

'I think this is the longest that we haven't seen each other since we moved into our flat. How long ago was that?'

'It must be six years ago,' said Anna. 'I can't believe it's taken me this long to visit you. I'd been thinking about it ever since you never came home but it's been five months now. I don't know where the time goes.'

She did know. There was no time when she was working. Or she never made time. She knew that now. Her priorities had been pretty skewed. Even when Rachel was still in London, it was rare that she'd see her outside of inviting her to something work-related.

'Well, you're here now.' Rachel paused then said, 'And how are things?'

'Same as when we spoke. I'm still fired, I still don't know what happened and I still don't know what to do.'

'Some time away is bound to help you get a bit of perspective and this place is special. Honestly, Anna, it'll help like you can't even believe. I still can't believe how my life has changed in the past six months. I don't feel as if I'm the same person that lived in London at all.'

Jonas looked into the rear-view mirror, catching Rachel's

eye and beaming at her. Anna wasn't sure she could take this level of lovey-doveyness if this was what they were like all the time. Whatever she thought of Adam, at least she didn't feel like a third wheel every time she was with him and Rachel. As happy as she was that her friend had found the love of her life, it might be hard to live with.

As the city began to take shape around them, Anna gazed out of the window, listening to Rachel point out various things to her before they pulled up on a tiny street amongst lots of tiny houses, all similar with coloured roofs and laid out very higgledy-piggledy with scraps of garden between them.

'Here we are!' said Rachel, climbing out of the jeep as Jonas held the door for her. He was a gentleman, which made a nice change.

Jonas carried Anna's case along a cobbled path towards a tiny house which was red with a grey roof. It hardly looked big enough for two people, let alone three of them.

'It's lovely,' Anna exclaimed when she walked through the door because it was. It was cosy and homely. Yes, bijou but somewhere that felt welcoming and suddenly Anna didn't mind that it might be a squash. She could see herself here. She knew it was Jonas's house, but she could see Rachel's touch in everything, and it felt like her friend's house too.

'We sleep on the mezzanine,' Rachel said pointing to where a steep ladder led to a platform in the vaulted roof of the main room. We've made Jonas's office into a room for you.

Rachel led the way through the tiny kitchen to a room that was completely filled with a bed. The room was clad in wood which had been painted white and there was a tiny window that overlooked one of the little garden spaces. There were shelves of books and one shelf lower down that had a tiny bedside light and room for a glass of water.

'I hope it's okay. At least it's your own space.'

'I love it, thank you.' Anna felt overcome with the emotion of seeing her friend and the feeling of someone caring for her. It had been a long time since she'd visited her parents - the only other place that would have that for her - and she'd forgotten what it was like.

'There's room for your case under the bed but if you want to hang anything up you can use the cupboard over here.'

Anna quickly wiped her eyes while Rachel turned to open a cupboard which was mainly full of coats and other outdoor wear.

'Thanks, Rach.' She flung her arms around her friend and gave her a tight hug. This was just what she needed. It had been the best thing she could have done to come and visit.

'So can I borrow one of these coats and go for a walk?'

Anna made her way down the cobbled path to the street where she caught a glimpse of the sea between the buildings and headed in that direction. As she crossed the road, she could see Snug, the shop that Rachel used to work for, just along the street and couldn't resist going in for a look. Every branch of Snug was a little bit different because it had its core stock the same as all the other branches, but they also sourced products from local designers and Anna was keen to see what Iceland had to offer.

If she hadn't known what to expect, the window would have drawn her in anyway. There was a huge sofa in there which had some amazing colourful woollen throws artfully arranged across it along with a couple of lamps on the floor which Anna would have purchased on the spot if it wasn't for having to get them home.

'Welcome to Snug,' one of the assistants said as she walked in. That was weird. Why were they speaking English before they knew whether she was English? Maybe she looked English.

She smiled and began to wander around the store. There

were some gorgeous, scented candles with sprigs of heather embedded in the translucent wax and a range of glassware made from lava which was dark and glossy but somehow different to regular glass. But what caught her eye was a wooden rail which was heavy with lots of the throws she'd seen in the window. The colours were subtle and beautiful, and Anna knew she just had to have one. Choosing took some time. One had a thread of hot pink running through it, but another had a deep mustard which was one of her favourite colours at the moment.

'Do you need any help?' It was a smiling woman who looked oddly familiar.

'Not unless you can find me one of these throws that is a mash-up of all of the ones on this rail.' Anna momentarily forgot that the woman may not speak enough English to understand her. 'Sorry. It's hard to choose,' she said.

The woman laughed. 'Wait a second.'

She headed over to the window and pulled one of the throws from the sofa.

'I think this is what you're looking for.'

'Oh my god. It is the perfect one. You're a genius, thank you.'

'You're welcome. You're not Anna, are you?' She made a face as she said it as if apologising in advance if she was wrong.

'I am. So, I guess maybe you're Gudrun?'

'Welcome to Reykjavik,' said Gudrun giving her a quick hug. 'I didn't expect to meet you so soon.'

'I remember you from the photo Rachel sent me of the night she decided to stay here. You were at the lagoon place together?'

'Yes! Wow, that was a night to remember. So how are you finding it so far?'

'It's colder than I thought.'

Gudrun laughed. 'I think Rachel is used to it now. It is warmer in London in September, and she forgot to tell you.'

'I think it's always warmer in London. I had to borrow this coat because mine is a September-in-London kind of coat.' Anna couldn't quite believe she was having this conversation with a near stranger.

'You are probably right. Anyway, you will get used to it. You would like to take the throw?'

'Definitely. Thank you.'

'It is a great choice. They are one of Rachel's favourites in the store. She is visiting the workshop of Eldey, the weaver, on her tours.'

'It's such a great idea. I'm looking forward to giving her a hand with the marketing.'

'Yes, of course. That is why you came,' said Gudrun. Was it Anna's imagination or was she smirking?

'Actually, I'd love to get Rachel and Jonas a gift, like a moving-in-together present. Can you suggest something? You probably know the things she likes best in here.'

'I have something that might be perfect, and she hasn't seen it yet.'

Gudrun went over to a table near the back of the store and picked up a beautiful ceramic serving bowl. It was white with flecks of the softest pinks and greens in the glaze.

'She has two plates from the same potter, and I know she would love this.'

'It's a great choice, thanks.'

'I expect I will see you later at the bar,' said Gudrun as she packed up Anna's purchases.

'Great, see you!' She was happy to go along with whatever plans Rachel had made and was looking forward to seeing Gudrun again.

She left the store and headed back to Rachel's, forgetting that she had been heading down to the sea before she'd got side-tracked. It felt great to be here. It was weird because even though she'd never been to Reykjavik before, it felt familiar to her. Maybe that's why Rachel loved it so much. Perhaps that's how she fell so quickly for Jonas. For the first time in a while, life felt good.

5

Rachel was thrilled with the serving bowl, just as Gudrun had predicted.

'Oh, I wish I'd come with you! I wanted to be there when you two met. I knew you'd hit it off.' Rachel sat on Anna's bed, caressing the new throw that Anna had spread on there as she spoke, making Anna think that she might have to hide it before Rachel fell in love with it.

'Well, there was nothing to see so you didn't miss anything. She said we're going out tonight?'

'Only if you want to. It's completely up to you, if you're tired, we can go tomorrow instead.'

'Tonight's fine,' Anna said, finally beginning to unpack her suitcase which was in the kitchen as there wasn't space for it in her bedroom.

There were a couple of spare shelves in her room, so she managed to fold quite a lot of her clothes onto there along with other bits and pieces. Some things were hung in the kitchen cupboard and Rachel made a space in the tiny bathroom for her toiletries.

'Where's Jonas?' Anna wondered out loud. The house was small enough that you could tell whether someone was there or not even if they weren't in the same room.

'He's doing a Northern Lights excursion tonight, but the forecast isn't good, so he'll be back in time to go to the pub. Anyway, what do you think so far?'

'I think I can see why you decided to stay.'

'I knew you would. And how about Jonas?' Rachel looked shyly at Anna, obviously keen for confirmation that her boyfriend was hot and whatever else.

'He makes you happy, Rach, I can see that. And he's good-looking, too outdoorsy for me but I can see that he's attractive despite that.'

Rachel biffed Anna with a cushion. 'That's one of his best features, being outdoorsy!'

'Alright! But remember how weird that seems to me knowing London Rachel better than I know Reykjavik Rachel. You'd never been out with anyone who wore anything except a pair of brogues and a suit before.'

Rachel rolled her eyes. 'I know. London Rachel was an idiot.'

'No, she wasn't. She just needed to come here to find herself,' said Anna gently. 'And to get away from Adam.'

'Do you ever see him around?'

'From time to time. Not to talk to. Not that he'd talk to me anyway after he caught me packing up your stuff when he came back from work early.'

'That was a big ask. Thank you again for doing that for me. I just couldn't face leaving Jonas behind even to come back and sort everything out. I owe you a favour.'

'You're returning it now, Rach. This is just what I needed. I feel better already, and I've only been here a few hours.'

'You needed a break. I was trying to think of the last time you went on holiday, and I couldn't. Not since we went to Corfu for a week and that was before I moved in with Adam.'

'I take time off, I just never fancied the idea of going anywhere by myself,' she said defensively. 'And I don't remember you taking a holiday either. You can't count going to your parents.'

Rachel shrugged. 'Fair enough.'

'Have they met Jonas yet?' Rachel's mum was sure to love Jonas.

'Yes. They came over for a week as soon as I decided to stay. Obviously, they stayed in a hotel otherwise I don't think Jonas and I would still be together.'

'And they loved him, I bet. He comes out well against Adam.'

'Exactly. Plus, Jonas gets on with everyone. Even my dad got chatty.'

Rachel stood up and opened the lid of Anna's case. 'So, if this is empty now I could… oh, you kept that quiet!'

She pulled out the copy of Hey! magazine that Anna had bought at the airport but then couldn't quite bring herself to look at it. She'd left it in the case so that she didn't have to think about it.

Anna watched in silence as Rachel began flicking through to get to the spread about Freddie and Sophia's wedding.

'Oh, look at her dress. It's gorgeous, isn't it? And Freddie looks so dapper in that suit with his hair all smart. I can't believe you were there! Do you think you're in any of them?'

Rachel finally looked up and closed the magazine as soon as she saw Anna's face.

'I'm sorry. I wasn't thinking. You know what I'm like about stuff like this. Let's chuck it away.'

'No, it's okay. You keep it. You probably don't see many of those anymore.'

'Too right. Not without paying five times the cover price. Thanks.'

'It's stupid. It was a great wedding apart from the drone business. I was excited about seeing the photos and then… '

'It's not stupid, it's completely understandable. You've had a horrible time because of what happened here,' Rachel said, waving the magazine. 'It's natural to feel weird when you see a reminder of it.'

'I think going to the bar tonight is a great idea, you know. I haven't been out since… then. I could do with a drink.'

'Brilliant! It'll be like old times but with expensive drinks instead of free ones.'

The evening in Íslenski Barinn was the best night out Anna had had in a long time. Rachel and Jonas's friends were a lively bunch and so welcoming. She was taken aback at how flawless their English was, although after a few drinks there was the odd word being uttered in Icelandic once they were too relaxed to wrack their brains for a decent translation.

Anna lay in bed now, exhausted from the day and tired from the alcohol but unable to give in to sleep. It was so quiet compared to London, although she could hear the hushed voices of Rachel and Jonas along with the murmur of laughter which made her smile. Through the window, she could see the fairy lights that were twirled around the branches of the tree in the tiny garden. It was comforting and relaxing and she felt a warmth inside her that she hadn't noticed for a long time.

She woke with a start. It was still dark, but someone was up and the door between her and the kitchen did nothing to dampen the noise of them trying to do something quietly. From where she lay, she reached and pulled the door open a tiny bit. Jonas was stirring something in a pan on the stove with his other hand ready on the burner knob to catch the kettle before it began to whistle. She rubbed her eyes, sat up and pulled on a sweatshirt and some joggers before emerging into the kitchen.

'Morning, Jonas.'

'Anna, I'm sorry for waking you.'

'It's fine. What time is it?'

'Six o'clock,' he said with a rueful smile. 'Would you like a coffee?'

'That'd be great, thanks.'

She sat at the table and watched Jonas spoon some porridge into a bowl, declining when he offered her some but wrapping her hands around the hot mug of coffee when he placed it in front of her.

'Where are you going on your excursion?' she asked.

'It is a hike to a waterfall. It's only possible in the months when there is no snow. Soon we will be back to winter activities. Would you like to come?'

'Oh, no thanks. Maybe another time.' She smiled, thinking that although it seemed a shame not to see more of the country, hiking to a waterfall wasn't her idea of fun. Whereas she was excited to get stuck into helping Rachel with her marketing.

'Anytime. Perhaps it is better to start with a visit to a hot pool. Relaxing and more of a holiday excursion,' he grinned.

'That does sound more appealing than hiking.'

'Ask Rachel. She knows some places to go.'

He finished his porridge, rinsed the bowl in the sink and then rummaged in the kitchen cupboard for his coat.

'I will see you tonight.'

He left the house and Anna wondered what to do now that she was up so early, and Rachel was still asleep. In London, she might have got dressed and gone out for breakfast but was anywhere likely to be open at this time in the morning in Reykjavik?

Switching the joggers for jeans, Anna decided to go for a walk to see. She remembered the spare key that Rachel had given her the day before and borrowed the same coat that she'd worn yesterday.

It shouldn't have been a surprise that at that time in the

morning when the sun was just beginning to rise, it was colder than it had been yesterday. Before she locked the door behind her, she went back inside to the kitchen cupboard and grabbed a woolly hat that she had an inkling Rachel might have knitted and pulled it on, grimacing at the slight scratchiness of it against her forehead but preferring that to brain freeze.

She locked the door and wandered down the cobbled path to the street, taking the same route that she had the day before. She knew that Snug was on one of the main roads in the city so thought wandering along there might prove fruitful. It wasn't long before she came across a bakery that was open and had the most delicious-looking array of pastries in the window and a hugely appealing aroma coming from inside.

Anna pushed the door open. A long glass and marble counter ran along one side of the shop and there were tables and seats nearer the back. It was simply furnished but the wooden tables and white chairs brought that feeling of Scandinavian cosiness to the place.

'Góður morgunn '

Anna smiled shyly. 'Góður morgunn,' she repeated, pretty sure of what she was saying.

'Can I help?'

Anna chose a cinnamon swirl and ordered a coffee then sat down at one of the tables. There was just one other person there, their pastry sat untouched while they wrote intensely in a notebook. It was an odd sight when these days everyone used laptops in coffee shops and who was working at this time in the morning anyway?

She pulled off her hat and laid it on the table. As she shrugged her coat off as well, the man at the other table caught her eye, and then looked away. Not writing now but pretending to. He looked slightly familiar, and Anna wondered whether she'd met him in the bar the night before, so the next time he looked up she smiled at him.

Once her pastry arrived, she was lost in the cinnamony sugary goodness of it when she felt his eyes on her again. It was annoying. If he knew her, why wouldn't he just say hello?

'Morning, great pastries,' she said, thinking that even if he was Icelandic his English would probably stretch to understanding that.

He nodded then went back to staring at his notebook.

Anna laughed to herself — what a weirdo — and went back to enjoying her breakfast. When she'd finished, she bought a few more pastries to take back for breakfast with Rachel but knowing that her friend would still be fast asleep, headed down to the sea on her way back.

The skies were blue and clear but there was a cold wind coming across the sea towards the path that separated the water from the city. Where Rachel lived, the houses were close together and it made for a cosy feel to the centre of the old town. Here by the sea, everything was open to the elements, with views of the mountains across the water and it felt more exposed and wilder, somehow. A strange feeling considering that there was a city just behind her.

Anna strolled along the path, towards a huge glass building that looked a bit out of place but quite majestic, nevertheless. Beyond it, she could see a harbour so she headed in that direction where the road wound back into the town and she had a sense that if she carried on, she would be back near where she'd started.

She stopped to cross the road, looking both ways quite carefully given that the traffic was the wrong way around. The man from the bakery was behind her. Some way off but there was no mistaking him with the black-framed glasses he wore. He was bundled up in a huge puffer coat and a beanie hat. It was surely a coincidence that he was following her. If she crossed the road and he did too, then she'd start to worry.

She crossed but didn't look back until she'd reached the corner of a street which gave her a bit of cover. Once she'd walked purposefully around the corner, she pressed herself to the wall and peeked around. He hadn't followed her, thank goodness but was carrying on, heading towards the harbour.

Anna laughed at herself. It was so ridiculous to think that someone was following her. It was broad daylight in a city a hundred times safer than London. Get a grip.

6

Ned was sure it was her. The woman from the wedding who had oddly made an impression on him despite their brief meeting. She'd obviously seen him looking at her and then when she tried to make conversation, he just froze. Whether that was a symptom of being in Iceland where he hadn't spoken to another soul for a couple of weeks or whether it was some kind of strange effect she had on him, he wasn't sure. Either way, it was embarrassing.

Her hair was wavier than he remembered but the image of her on Freddie's wedding day was so ingrained in his mind, that he knew it was her. Why didn't he just take her conversation opener and run with it?

He watched her cross the road near the Harpa concert hall and was fairly certain that she clocked him, so he decided not to follow her back into town and instead carried on towards his apartment. Would he see her again and if he did would he be brave enough to introduce himself? It was the first time he could remember worrying about anything like this. Normally he met women when he was with the lads. Usually, the women they mixed with were known to someone whether it was their management, PR team or record label. Jeannie was the assistant to their publicist. It was the safest way to keep things inside the circle but at the same time, he'd never felt a spark of attraction for anyone he'd met like that, not even Jeannie if he was honest. And that was how he knew that the woman from the wedding had had such an effect on him. She was beautiful, funny and capable and he'd longed to run into her again, but she'd not been at the wedding reception, and he didn't want Sophia getting wind of anything, which was why even though he could easily have asked Freddie to find out her identity, he hadn't.

It seemed so unlikely that she would be here, in Reykjavik of all places. He smiled as he let himself into his apartment and pulled off his coat and hat, ruffling his hat hair. If it was her and it was meant to be, he'd see her again.

These early mornings were a revelation to him. When he was in London, there was always something going on, invariably meaning that he'd have a drink most nights and sleep in most mornings. Here, he had laid off the booze since drinking alone seemed like a bad idea and after a couple of days, he realised he enjoyed the feeling of waking up feeling relatively fresh. After a few days his natural rhythm had kicked in and he'd started going to bed around ten and waking around six.

Since he'd arrived in Reykjavik, Ned had found the pace of life suited him. No one had recognised him yet, helped by the fact that he'd forgotten to pack his contacts and was wearing his glasses all the time, something that the public had never seen when he was in the band. For some reason glasses had been seen unfavourably by the stylists the band had used but now, there were no rules and every tiny change felt like a huge step towards independence.

He tossed his notebook onto the sofa next to his guitar. Over the past week, he seemed to have fallen into a routine of writing lyrics while he had breakfast at the bakery — the only place that was open when he woke up — followed by playing the guitar and trying to make some sense out of it for most of the rest of the day. It stunned him how easily he had left his life behind. The life he'd lived every day for the past ten years. After leaving the band he had started to think that he was going to still be living the same life but just alone rather than with his bandmates, his friends. That they'd be going on with that life and he'd be a shadow beside them, not knowing how to move away. It had been starting to feel a bit like that before he'd decided to leave London for a while, and it was relief that he'd managed to break that habit.

He made himself a coffee and sat in his favourite chair, a comfy sheepskin-covered one that he relaxed into to watch the city slowly waking up. On his walk that morning he'd seen a bar advertising live music. He was craving something like that. It was all very well taking advantage of the solitude to write, and it was going pretty well, but he missed being around music. Missed jamming with Freddie, the only other member of The Rush who could play an instrument and perhaps one of the reasons that they were so close.

Could he go to something like that? Based on a couple of weeks of being here he was sure no one would recognise him. As far as he knew the press hadn't cottoned on to the fact that he was in Reykjavik so from that point of view he could relax. Was it weird going to something like that alone? Was he going to manage the next almost three months here alone not speaking to anyone? He grinned to himself. Before he quit the band, that scenario would have seemed like a dream. It was easy to get comfortable in another reality and forget that it was what you'd wanted.

He picked up his phone and called Freddie.

'Mmmm.'

Ned realised as soon as he heard Freddie that he'd forgotten it was still only around eight in the morning. Far too early for him to be up unless he had to be.

'Sorry, man. It's me. I'll call back later.'

'S'okay. I'm awake now.' Ned could hear the shuffling sounds of Freddie getting out of bed and leaving the bedroom. 'How's it going in the land of ice and fire?'

'Yeah, good. I've been writing and some of it's decent, I think.'

'That's great.' The coffee machine fired up in Freddie's kitchen.

'This is going to sound weird. I think I've forgotten what normal is, Fred.'

'And you think I can help? Freddie laughed.

'I'm thinking of going to a bar to listen to some music. I think it's a guitar player.'

'Right...'

'Is that weird, going to something like that by myself?' He felt like an idiot for asking, but he needed to get someone else's take on it. It was a long time since he'd made any decisions about how wise it would be to go somewhere or not.

'I don't think so. I mean, have you met anyone you could go with?'

'Making friends with strangers isn't my forte.'

'Just go, man. What's the worst that can happen?'

Getting recognised would be at the top of his list but he was pretty confident on that score.

'People think I'm sad?'

Freddie roared with laughter down the phone, making Ned smile and realise that it probably was as ridiculous a thing to worry about as Freddie thought it was.

'Sad? Come on Neddy boy, do you really think people are sitting around looking at who's there and making judgements on whether they should have rocked up with someone else? No one cares!'

'Brutal. But thanks.'

'Look, you forget you're in a different place now. A place where you can be an ordinary guy who loves music and wants to go out to a bar and enjoy it. You're that guy. Stop worrying about everyone else.'

'Thanks, Fred. I needed that.'

'And never ring me before ten in the morning. I thought you knew better.'

'Lazy arse,' said Ned affectionately, then hung up.

Ned's heart was beating so fast he thought he'd have to turn round and go home just to calm himself down. He was surprised how nervous he was given that he'd decided, quite definitely, that it was a good idea. There was some part of him that hadn't got that message.

He took a deep breath and walked up the steps into the bar. It wasn't that busy but then it was a Wednesday night. He walked straight up to the bar and ordered half a litre of beer. Once he'd taken a couple of swigs, he felt more relaxed and surveyed the place for somewhere to sit, settling on an unoccupied table for two in a dark corner with a good view of the musician.

He tried to relax into it. Resisted the urge to pull out his phone to make himself look busy. Instead, he took in his surroundings, enjoyed his beer and waited for the music to start.

After five minutes or so, close to the time it was due to start, the place started to fill. A bearded man said something to him in Icelandic and gestured to the spare chair at his table to which Ned nodded and did the international gestures for 'please take the chair, I don't need it,' and was a little taken aback when the guy, rather than taking the chair, sat down at Ned's table. He was alone as well and that heartened Ned and bizarrely seemed to endorse his decision to come. The man smiled at Ned, then turned his chair towards the musician, his beer on the table resting in his left hand.

The music was great, melodic and heartfelt with Icelandic lyrics that sounded beautiful even though Ned obviously couldn't understand them. The guy played well and was a pleasure to listen to. Once Ned had finished his beer, he felt brave and tapped his table mate on the arm, picked up his empty glass and gestured to the bar.

'Drink?'

'*Takk*,' said the man and pointed to the brewery logo on his empty glass to indicate which beer he wanted.

Ned gave him a nod and went to the bar feeling immensely pleased with himself for being so brave and normal.

His drinking buddy gave him a grateful nod when he went back to the table and held his glass up towards the musician.

'*Frábær tónlist!*' he said, which Ned could tell meant that he thought it was great and nodded and smiled in agreement.

Once the music was over, everyone applauded enthusiastically, and Ned stood up with everyone else in appreciation.

He downed the last of his drink and went to pull his coat on when his new friend gestured that he'd buy another round.

He'd come this far. What was the worst that could happen? And two beers in, another one was a welcome thought. He nodded and sat back down. But now that the music was over, they were going to have to talk. The guy was obviously Icelandic, and Ned wasn't sure if he could manage the length of time it took to drink half a litre of beer talking in gestures.

'Thanks,' he said when the guy came back to the table. He picked up the glass and gestured cheers to him.

'*Skál!*'

'*Skál!*' Ned replied.

'You are English?'

'Yes,' Ned said with some relief. 'Ned.' He held out his

hand.

'Brun.' He took Ned's hand and gave it a single, sturdy shake. 'Are you on holiday?'

'Sort of a working holiday,' said Ned.

'What do you do?'

'Similar to that guy, actually.' Ned gestured to where the musician was packing up his things.

'Wow. Guitar?'

'Yes. Do you play?'

'Very badly,' said Brun with a grin. 'I learned to impress girls,' he said with a rueful smile. 'It's not really in here.' He tapped his chest with his hand.

'Did it work?'

Brun nodded. 'Yes, although she will also tell you that I am very bad.'

They both laughed.

'What do you do?'

'I work for a tour company, running excursions. You know, Northern Lights, hiking, all of that.'

'That's cool. I haven't been outside the city yet. What's your most popular tour?'

'The Golden Circle is very popular. Takes in the geyser and the national park, all the best tourist things. We are called Iceland Adventures, easy to remember.'

'Great, I'll look into that. So, are there any other places that have live music around here?'

Brun laughed. 'How long have you been here, my friend? It is everywhere.'

'I don't get out much,' said Ned, with a grin.

'Working too hard?'

'Something like that.'

Brun pulled a card out of his pocket. 'I will be going to a place on Friday with some friends. A great guitarist and singer are playing. You are welcome to call me and come along.'

When Ned left the bar, waving to Brun who was heading in the opposite direction, he felt on top of the world. This was what normal was.

7

Thankfully Jonas wasn't out at the crack of dawn every morning and Anna was grateful for the lie-ins, although she had already planned to go back to the bakery on Laugavegur the next time she was awake early enough. The stalker guy was niggling her and when she'd told Rachel, she'd laughed and reassured her that despite the prolific amount of crime fiction set in Iceland, it was the safest place in the world, and he had probably been coincidentally going in the same direction or he liked her and was trying to build up the courage to speak.

At a more civilised hour of the day, Rachel had taken Anna to her favourite coffee shop, Te & Kaffi which was just a few doors down from Snug. Rachel had apparently spent a lot of time in there when she'd first arrived in Reykjavik.

'Just because you met Jonas within an hour of arriving here, I don't think you should assume that's normal.'

'I'm just saying. You thought he was nice, he might have been thinking the same.'

She *had* told Rachel he looked nice. He had brown hair which had been pretty messy, but Anna blamed that on the hat-hair that everyone here had to live with unless they wanted to freeze to death, and his glasses did it for her too.

He'd not shaved for a few days which she quite liked as well.

'Mmm. He was nice. But how much can you tell about someone you meet in a bakery and don't talk to? I mean, I spoke to him so maybe he didn't understand English, in which case we've got no future anyway.'

Rachel laughed. 'Well, it's always nice to see someone who makes you think… you know.'

'Makes you think you're not dead inside after all?'

'I'm just saying it's not often that you think anyone is worth a second look. You're very hard to please when it comes to men.'

'No.' Anna put down the chunk of muffin she was just about to eat. 'I'm not hard to please, I just have high standards and I can't be bothered putting the time into a relationship with someone when you can tell at the beginning that it's not going to last.'

'I think you've made my point for me, thank you.'

'That's not being hard to please. I'm just good at sorting the wheat from the chaff at a very early stage.'

Rachel choked on her coffee. 'You're a classic commitment-phobe! You hook up with guys and that's all, it never goes any further.'

Anna couldn't disagree and didn't think it would help her argument to point out that one of these hook-ups had become a regular hook-up, which surely counted towards being a relationship even if technically wasn't. Dom was a writer for one of the online magazines about the newest, hottest places to go in London, so he was quite often at the same events as her. It was easy, she liked him but there were no strings. In many ways, he was the perfect man.

'Well, either way, I don't need a holiday romance with someone who couldn't even be bothered to pretend to understand me. I didn't come for that kind of distraction, I came for the more work-related distraction of helping you with your marketing and we haven't even discussed it since I arrived.'

Rachel looked sheepish.

'What? Have you changed your mind?'

'No, not exactly. I just really wanted you to come, and I knew that the promise of something like that would encourage you. But I'm pretty much sorted, I think.'

Anna's first instinct was to be annoyed with Rachel but having been in Iceland for a couple of days, she was getting a feel for the place and quite enjoying her holiday. So, if that's all it turned out to be, perhaps that was okay after all.

'Well, you should have been honest. I'm not an idiot. You could have just been bossy and told me to get my arse over here because what else was I going to do?'

'As if being bossy has ever worked with you. But I'm sorry. I just thought you'd need a better reason than that I wanted to see you and show you where I live now.'

Rachel was right. Staying in London, jobless, wasn't going to help her decide what was going to happen next and coming to Iceland had given her something to do at least. Now that she was here, it had started to give her a bit more perspective on her life in London. It had shown her that not everything revolved around the PR scene within a West End postcode and that her life in London had been exactly that. Only that.

'I'm glad I came, Rach, marketing to do or not. But I'd love to see what your plans are.'

They spent another hour or so chatting about Rachel's plans for her new business. She was taking parties of tourists to visit some of the local artisan craftspeople in their workshops; an idea that came to her when she'd had a hand in sourcing some of the stock for the Snug store. It was a bonus that Jonas owned a tour company, so she didn't have to invest in things like vehicles. Jonas had a couple of extra minibuses that he used for Northern Lights excursions, but she could book the use of them during the day, so it was perfect.

'And we can always tag a visit to a hot pool onto the back of a workshop visit and there are even some artists willing to run hands-on workshops for guests.'

'It's total genius,' Anna said, proud of her friend for starting such a niche business that had the bones of being something amazing. 'So do you have a website or anything?'

'Not really. I've got a page on the Iceland Adventures website, and I think that'll be enough for now because I want the groups to be small so that I can run it by myself.'

'But what if Jonas's customers aren't interested in craft stuff? His customers aren't necessarily yours and vice versa.'

'Gudrun is putting the word out in Snug because I have a few of their suppliers on my tours. If someone buys one of the blankets like the one you got, she'll give them a leaflet about the tour.'

'That's a great idea. But what if it's their last day and they only just found out about you.'

'Look, Anna, I know you want to get stuck into something, but I think I'm where I need to be at the moment.'

'Okay, don't get defensive. I know it's your baby, I'm trying to make you think about it differently, that's all. You've got your product and it's brilliant, no one else is doing it. You just need the right kind of people to know about it before they get here.'

'You're right. I suppose,' said Rachel rolling her eyes. 'What do you think I need to do?'

Anna grinned. She loved this kind of thing. Getting the word out to the right people was what she excelled at.

'You give me some of those leaflets and leave it to me.'

'Okay you're on but that's enough work for today. If I learned anything from moving here it's that work-life balance is the key to happiness. We're going on an excursion.'

Anna's heart sank. 'Not something hikey?'

'No, something relaxing and you'll love it.'

A couple of hours later, Anna was immersed in steaming geothermal water with a cold beer in her hand thinking that aside from the naked showering which was compulsory before they could get into the pool, this was going to rank as the best experience of her holiday. The ten-minute car journey might rank as the worst; Rachel barely ever drove in the UK so being on the other side of the road was a challenge, but that was a distant memory now.

The Sky Lagoon was on the edge of an old harbour area on the outskirts of Reykjavik and was surrounded by high walls of black lava rock, but the infinity edge of the pool melted into a stunning vista of the Atlantic and gave Anna the feeling that she was part of the sea. The swim-up bar was a bonus as was the feeling of every tiny part of her being warm for the first time in a while.

'This place is amazing, Rach.'

'We only came for the first time a few weeks ago. It's quite new and Jonas wanted to see whether he could start offering it as part of a trip.'

'Well, *you* could. Let Jonas stick to the energetic stuff and you can do the relaxing side of things.'

'Mmm,' said Rachel, her eyes closed as she savoured the warmth. 'Good idea.'

'It's so funny, Rach. The last time I saw you, you were still with Adam, had been for years and now you're with someone completely different and it's so right. It just shows you can go for so long thinking you're happy... and imagine if you hadn't come here?'

'I know. I think about that all the time. It feels like fate or something. And I know this is weird but that's why I wanted you to come. This place... there's something that happens here. It's what you needed, Anna. Just to break out and see what else life could offer.'

'No offence, Rach. I'm having a great time, but I can't see myself living somewhere that requires so much thought about how many layers you need to survive leaving the house.'

'It's the summer, Anna,' Rachel laughed. 'Imagine what it was like when I came in February. There was snow everywhere and it was bloody freezing but I loved it like that.'

Rachel paused and looked at Anna until she caught her eye.

'What? You're looking at me funny.'

'I've got something to tell you.'

Anna grinned, feeling like a teenager. 'Go on then.'

'Me and Jonas are getting married.'

Anna threw her arms around her friend with such enthusiasm that she created a mini tsunami in the otherwise tranquil pool. 'Oh my god! When did he propose? Why didn't you tell me?'

'Officially it was when my parents came over but for us, it was at the Secret Lagoon when I decided to stay. It wasn't a proposal in the sense of 'Will you marry me?' but we both feel like that's when we decided.'

'I can't believe you haven't told me until now, Rach. That's amazing. He is such a great guy.'

Rachel beamed. 'I know. And again, this is going to sound odd but we're getting married in November. Will you stay until then?'

As much as Anna wanted to blurt out that yes, she would love to stay. The thought of staying in Rachel's cramped spare room for another two months was overwhelming.

'I don't think I can, Rach. I'll come back for the wedding, obviously.'

Rachel burst out laughing. 'I knew you'd say that! I told Jonas! Oh, Anna. You must be sick to death of sleeping in that tiny room, getting woken up at the crack of dawn when Jonas goes to work.'

It was so confusing. 'It's fine for a holiday but you're right. I can't live like that for two months. And anyway, I need to get back to London.'

'For what?'

Anna couldn't answer that because they both knew there was nothing to pull her home.

'Okay, you win. I can't live at your house for two months. It'll drive me crazy. Sorry.'

'We have a solution.' Rachel's eyes were shining. 'Jonas and I have bought a house together so we thought we'd move out and you can stay in our old house until after the wedding.'

Now that was a more tempting prospect. She loved Rachel and Jonas's house with its cosy feel and if she was there by herself, she'd get to sleep on the mezzanine which was unreasonably exciting for a thirty-two-year-old woman.

'Are you sure? I can pay you something for it.'

But Rachel shook her head. 'No, we're completing on our new place next week and haven't even put it on the market yet. And it'd do us a favour if you could maybe help out if there's a viewing?'

'Of course. Blimey. Thanks, Rach. It's really generous of you both.'

'Generous or selfish, because you're the chief bridesmaid and I need a hand to plan the wedding.'

8

Ned had ummed and ahhed about ringing Brun ever since he'd handed over his card in the bar. It was totally out of his realm of experience, for the past ten years at least, to call a complete stranger out of the blue. Okay, Brun had offered to take Ned to the gig on Friday, but it didn't stop the paranoia surfacing to make Ned wonder whether he'd meant it. Had he felt sorry for him because he was alone? Had he recognised him?

That thought snapped him out of it and made him laugh out loud because Brun didn't look like your typical The Rush fan with his thick beard and stocky physique. And besides, Brun had been there alone so how could he pity Ned for being there by himself? And like he kept trying to remind himself, he had nothing to lose.

'Hey Brun,' he said once Brun had picked up and announced himself. 'It's Ned from the bar the other night.'

'Hello! I was wondering if you were going to call. Are you coming out tonight?'

'If that's okay. Should I meet you there?'

'It's hard to find. We will be in Íslenski Barrin, the bar from the other night, first. Meet us there at eight.'

'Great, see you then'

Ned exhaled. He felt pleased with himself. It was a bit of a milestone because he was so used to other people organising his life, almost all aspects of it. It felt great to be in control.

He spent the rest of the day looking forward to having something planned for once. Something that he wanted to do rather than something he had to. One thing he wasn't missing was going to event after promotion after awards ceremony, mixing with people who only knew him as Ned Nokes from The Rush. Because that wasn't who he was at all, but he'd been that person for so long that it was hard to remember that no one here knew who he was. Here he was Ned. A guy who loved live music and was here to write some songs.

He hesitated at the bottom of the steps that led into the bar. Suddenly he didn't think he remembered Brun well enough to recognise him. What if he walked in and he was first? He had made sure not to get here before eight and now it was ten past. Okay, he'd go in, walk straight to the bar and order a drink and then look around for Brun while he waited.

Unsurprisingly the place was packed, as were most bars in any city on a Friday night. His plan faltered for a second as he had to shuffle between people to get to the bar but as he did so, he spotted Brun on a large table next to the windows that overlooked the street. There were plenty of drinks on the table, so Ned felt safe in the knowledge that he'd have time to get himself one before they left for the gig. In a bid to settle his nerves, as well as half a litre of beer he ordered a single shot of an Icelandic whisky that he spotted on a shelf of spirits behind the bar. He took a small sip just to assess whether it was a good option for another time when he might want to drink it for its own sake rather than neck it. He downed the rest with brief appreciation, then picked up his beer and headed over to the table.

Before he reached it, he saw her. The woman from the wedding. The woman he thought he'd seen in the bakery the other morning. He'd wanted to talk to her that morning, but he was sure she hadn't recognised him, and it seemed like a big step to put himself out there. Because she knew *that* Ned Nokes and he wasn't ready for that life to have caught up with him in Iceland.

But it looked like if he wanted to go out with Brun, he was going to have to let that happen because she was sitting at the same table.

He took a deep breath and walked over. Brun stood up and greeted him warmly as soon as he noticed.

'Hello, Ned!'

'Hey, Brun.' They shook hands, Ned counting down the seconds until he'd have to look her in the eye. And then everyone would know. His incognito trip to Iceland would be over.

'Guys, this is Ned. Ned this is Jonas, Rachel, Gudrun, Olafur, Anna and Kristin.

They all greeted him as he stood there smiling, waiting for her to recognise him.

'Sit down here,' said Gudrun pulling a stool out from under the table. 'Brun made us save it for you.'

'Thanks.'

The conversation carried on around him as he sipped his beer as slowly as he could, trying to combat the urge to down the whole thing and smiling in what he hoped were the right places. He looked at Anna, he was sure that was her name if he'd been keeping track properly when Brun was doing the introductions. She was chatting to the woman next to her and periodically sipped her beer. He'd kind of expected her to announce his identity to everyone and he was grateful that either she hadn't made the connection — although how many people were called Ned — or she was just biding her time.

'Drink up, guys!' Brun said a few minutes later. 'Time to go.'

Everyone busied themselves with finishing their drinks before pulling on coats, hats, gloves and whatever else they'd divested themselves of since they'd come inside.

Ned watched Anna, smiling when he heard her complain to Gudrun about the hat she was wearing being itchy and Gudrun telling her not to say anything to Rachel.

Once everyone was outside, breaking naturally out of the group to walk in their couples he assumed, it was easy to fall into step next to her.

'I saw you in the bakery,' he said.

'I spoke to you in the bakery, and you ignored me,' she retorted, quite correctly.

'Sorry about that. I was taken aback. I remembered you from the wedding, obviously,' he said, noticing that she tried to suppress a smile at that remark. 'But I thought it couldn't have been you, here in Reykjavik. And I didn't think you'd recognised me so, I don't know, I just panicked.'

'You're right. I didn't recognise you, but you did look familiar, just less… '

'Tidy?' he ventured, hoping she wasn't going to go for something more personal.

'Mmm. That's it exactly. Less tidy.'

She turned to him and smiled. Her blue eyes sparkled more than they had on Freddie's wedding day. And she looked less tidy too but in the best way possible. Her hair was in waves that settled around her shoulders and her cheeks glowed, probably from the cold, because she wasn't wearing much make-up as far as he could tell. Natural looked amazing on her.

'Thanks. I'll take that. All of that preening seems a bit unnecessary here, especially when you take your hat on and off twenty times a day?'

'Only twenty? You obviously don't go out much,' she said as she pushed her fingers underneath her hat to rub her forehead.

'Having trouble with your hat?'

'My friend knitted it for me, so I have to wear it,' she said, so seriously that he laughed out loud.

'Are you here visiting her?'

'Yes. I'm taking some time off work and it seemed like a good opportunity. She moved here a few months ago. And what are you doing here, Ned Nokes?'

'Same kind of thing. Having some downtime, doing some writing, hanging out with some of the locals.'

'It's so weird. Fancy you making friends with Brun and him knowing my friend.'

He sensed that she was almost going to say something else but was holding back. Was she about to say out loud that she'd thought about him since the wedding, or was that just wishful thinking?

'Did you see that photo of us that made the papers?'

'Yes, Rachel showed me. She's a huge celebrity gossip fan, she was all over the pictures of the wedding.'

'Does she know it's me?' A slight feeling of panic had risen in his chest at the words 'celebrity gossip fan'.

Anna picked up on that because she said, 'No, I don't think so. But you don't need to worry. She thinks Freddie's hotter than you.'

He laughed, loudly enough to cause Anna's friend to turn around and look at them in curiosity. 'Thanks for that dose of reality.'

'I'm just joking but relax. It'll be okay.' She nudged his arm gently with her elbow. 'These guys are nothing if not laid back. I think you've probably come to the right place if you want to stay under the radar.'

They had been following the rest of the group through the streets of Reykjavik, not paying any attention to where they were going as they chatted, but it was an area that Ned didn't recognise, and he began to feel uncomfortable again. They were in front of a utilitarian-looking building with no windows but once the sound of the music coming out of the open door reached him, it was more than enough to tempt him inside.

'Sounds good,' he said to Anna, a comment that was based on the fact that it was music rather than anything discernible that he could hear.

'Yep, Brun reckons they're the best thing to come out of Reykjavik in a while.'

They made their way inside where everyone was busy applauding the song that had just finished.

The singer, a woman with hair so blonde it was almost white, was speaking into the microphone in Icelandic, then everyone cheered, and she launched into the next song on the back of the guitar intro from the guy who was sitting to her right. He played so beautifully that Ned was mesmerised, and Anna had to pull on his sleeve to get him to sit down at the table that seemed to have materialised for them even though the place was packed.

Once that song was over, Ned took a second to look around the place. It was like an old-fashioned cabaret club that you might find in the UK; tables with little lamps on them, dark walls and swoops of velvet curtaining around the stage area, but with a modern twist that lifted it by the furniture not being dark mahogany stuff, but lighter, more natural oak and the seats were a cacophony of colours and types that made the place feel relaxed and like it wasn't taking itself too seriously.

Ned offered to go up and get the drinks but Brun's friend, Jonas, who was sitting on the other side of him, shook his head. 'They will come and take our order.'

'Cool,' said Ned, sitting back in his seat, enjoying the vibe of the place.

'Have you been in town long?' Jonas asked him in the gap between the next songs.

'A couple of weeks.'

'How are you finding it?'

'Great. Tonight has been amazing. Thanks for including me.'

Jonas smiled and shrugged. 'I love showing our country to visitors. The parts they would not normally see, especially.'

Ned nodded and then went back to listening attentively once the next song started.

The drinks were ordered and arrived along with some bowls of nibbles that someone had the foresight to add to the order and everyone was grateful for, then all too soon the music came to an end. Ned got to his feet with the rest of the table and clapped and whooped along with everyone else.

'Did I tell you?' Brun asked him across the table once they'd all sat down again.

'They were amazing, just sensational playing from that guy.'

'Indeed. There is another, slightly different band on next. Are we staying?' he asked everyone.

Gudrun and Kristin began talking to him in Icelandic and he put up his hands in defence. 'Yes, yes, we will stay then.'

Jonas leaned in. 'They love this next band, they do cover versions of songs and it is music they like to dance to.'

Ned nodded. 'Right.'

Jonas left the table to go and talk to someone across the other side of the room and Ned turned to Anna.

'Have you seen much of the place yet?'

'Not really, I went to a pool with Rachel but I'm not into hiking and all the stuff that Jonas and Brun do. How about you?'

'No, nothing. Until tonight I'd not ventured much further than the bakery. Seems like a shame not to see something of the country though.'

'How long are you going to stay?'

'Another couple of months, I think.'

'Me too. Oh, I love this song,' she said as the band that now stood on the stage struck up for their first number. 'Do you want to dance?'

Before he could answer, Anna had grabbed his hand and was pulling him behind her towards the stage where a few tables had been cleared to make a space. At least they weren't the only ones. Gudrun, Rachel and Kristin had followed them. They began dancing and Ned felt himself begin to relax as he watched Anna and the others dance, singing the chorus loudly to each other while they laughed and grinned with joy. Anna was quite something. Ned couldn't remember the last time he'd danced like this or been with a girl who danced like this. She was so carefree and happy, unaware of what anyone watching might think. So unlike the girls that hung around the VIP area of a club, watching him out of the corner of their eye to see if they were attracting his attention with their deliberate, carefully thought through moves.

A slower song came on and a few people sidled off the dance floor. Anna looked at him, questioningly. He had no hesitation in moving towards her and gently placing one hand on her waist, taking her other and holding it against his chest in a cross between a ballroom hold and a slow dance.

'Is this okay?' he asked.

She nodded, smiling. 'It's great.'

They moved to the music together, Ned feeling like all he wanted to do was gaze into her eyes but forcing himself to look across her shoulder because everything was feeling quite intense. Just before the end of the song, she leaned her head against his shoulder and he felt something rush through him, like a shot of adrenaline. It was just a dance. Get a grip.

The song ended and Anna pulled away from him with a

shy smile.

'Shall we get another drink?' she said and led him back towards the table as the next song started. It was the opening bars to The Rush's most famous song and Ned suddenly went from having one of the best nights out he'd had in a long time to thinking he might vomit. He felt as if everyone in the place was looking at him, somehow knowing that he was there.

He pulled his hand from Anna's and darted towards the chair where his coat was, the chair crashing over as he grabbed it.

'Sorry, I need to go,' he managed to say before he ran to the door and outside into the street.

9

Rachel mouthed, 'Where's he gone?' to Anna as she was getting dragged up to the dance floor by Gudrun.

Anna shrugged and motioned that she was going outside, grabbing her coat and pulling it on as she headed for the door. She was no rookie now; she was well in the habit of being properly attired every time she went outside.

Ned was along the street a little way, leaning against a wall and wrestling with the zip on his coat.

'Hey, Ned!'

He turned, acknowledging her but then began to walk away. 'Ned!' She caught up with him and stood in front of him, making him stop. 'Talk to me.'

He looked dreadful and she could tell he was struggling to get his breath.

'Did you think that song was rubbish?' she said, attempting to lighten the mood and distract him from whatever was causing this reaction.

He attempted a grim smile. 'It was just a shock. I thought everyone would realise it was me.'

'I think you probably need to work on realising that you're not the centre of attention anymore.' She took his hands in hers, without any thought as to whether he'd think that was an odd thing for her to do but when he squeezed hers in return, she felt a sudden connection between them.

'It's ridiculous,' he said, looking back at the door.

There was a look in his eye that made Anna realise that he thought people might be following him.

'It isn't ridiculous. I've worked with enough people like you to know that this stuff is hard. It's bad enough to cope with when you have a massive team of people around you but you're here by yourself. You're bound to feel vulnerable.'

She dropped one of his hands but kept hold of the other. He didn't let go either. They began to walk down the street, neither of them having any idea where they were or where they were going.

'They were actually doing a pretty good job of it,' he said, his voice sounding more relaxed.

'It's got to be weird hearing your song played by someone else.'

He shrugged. 'It's not as if me and the guys haven't seen bands massacre our songs before, not that that's what was happening in there tonight. It just took me by surprise, and I'd left before I could even think about what I was doing.'

He gave her a look that she knew meant he was considering how much to share with her about how he really felt. She said nothing, letting the silence allow him time to decide.

'It felt like my old life was back and kind of jumped out at me. I don't even know how to explain it and I feel like a complete idiot for running out of the bloody club. I mean, everyone's going to — '

'No one will think anything of it. They were all a few drinks in, and they'll just think you had enough and wanted to leave. It's no big deal.'

'Thanks, Anna.' They were still holding hands, but he took hers and tucked it into the crook of his arm. 'I'm going to walk you home.'

'If you know where that is, it's more than I do,' she laughed.

When Anna let herself into the house, having said goodbye to Ned on the main road to save him from getting any more lost than they'd already got tonight, Rachel was sitting on the sofa in the lounge reading a magazine. She pressed her finger to her lips and pointed to the kitchen.

Pulling the kitchen door closed behind them, she said, 'Sorry, Jonas is up early again tomorrow. I don't want to wake him, but I couldn't go to bed without finding out what was going on tonight! You seemed to hit it off with that guy Ned.'

Anna sighed. She was tired and the prospect of an early start for Jonas meant the same for her. 'Ned, Rach.' She waited for the penny to drop. It didn't take long and then Rachel was laughing and at the same time clamping her hand over her mouth in disbelief.

'Oh my god, Anna, it's Ned Nokes! And you met at the wedding! Did you know he was here?'

Anna shook her head. 'No, it was a total coincidence. I mean, we did see each other at the bakery the other day but I didn't realise it was him.'

'Well, no! I mean he looks nothing like his pictures. So, when did you realise? Was it tonight? Is that why you left with him?'

'I knew as soon as Brun introduced him to us. He's worried that everyone's going to be weird when they know who he is. Nobody here knows at all yet and I think he's enjoying being around people who don't know that he's Ned Nokes. You know he left the band and I think he might be struggling with it a bit.'

'Right, of course. It'll be easy to forget who he is because he looks so different.'

'You have to make the effort not to talk about any celebrity stuff with him, okay? Unless he brings it up first. I mean we need to be natural around him. Not weird.'

'No weirdness. That's fine. I can do that.'

Anna had no doubt of Rachel's good intentions, but she knew her friend's enthusiasm for celebrity gossip could get the better of her.

'And Rach, if Gudrun and Kristin don't know who he is, don't tell them. We have to try and give him the privacy he came here for.'

Rachel went to bed thrilled and swearing she'd be able to keep the secret. Anna went to bed thinking of Ned. She was surprised at how vulnerable he seemed. The press portrayed him as confident, and maybe he was normally, but not at the moment. Right now, it seemed to her that he didn't know himself at all. He needed to be surrounded by people he could trust so that he didn't have to deal with the pressure of wondering what people thought of him. She'd quickly realised that. It might have been naive of her to think she understood what he was going through but it was similar to what she was facing herself. Finding herself outside of everything she'd relied on for fulfilment in most aspects of her life. The only difference was that Ned had chosen that whereas it had been forced upon her, but the struggle to find your place in a world that didn't look the same as it had a few weeks ago, that was the same for both of them.

The next morning, Anna waited until she heard Jonas leave, then got herself up and dressed and quietly headed out to the bakery. She had no idea whether she'd find Ned there, but she needed to see him, to make sure he was okay.

It was a bright, cold morning. It seemed to be a little bit darker than when she'd left the house at the same time last week so maybe the days were getting shorter. They were certainly getting colder. She pulled her hat down over her hair which she'd brushed and then run some hair oil through to try and tame the worst of the frizz and pulled on her coat and a pair of gloves she'd had to borrow from the cupboard once she felt how cold it was.

The beckoning lights of the bakery warmed her before she even set foot inside and the smell of the freshly baked goods was as amazing as it had been the last time she'd visited. She greeted the woman behind the counter in Icelandic, a little more confidently this time, ordered a custard danish and a coffee and went to sit down. Her heart was beating hard as she realised how much she was hoping to see Ned there.

And there he was. His head was bent over the table, and she could see the top of his pen wriggling around as he wrote furiously into his notebook. She was reluctant to disturb him, so perched on the first chair she came to waiting for a lull.

The words were obviously flowing so she ended up eating her breakfast alone, staring at his back, when she'd hoped to be sharing it with him. Once she'd finished her coffee, she realised that the lull was never going to come. Instead, she opened Google translate on her phone and translated 'Please could I have a pen and paper?' into Icelandic. She went up to the counter and showed the screen to the woman who laughed kindly before ripping a sheet of paper off her order pad and handing it to Anna with a pen.

'*Takk.*'

Then she wrote again into Google translate, 'Please can I buy him another drink, whatever he had before.' She showed her phone again, pointing to Ned.

The woman nodded and made a coffee. Anna wrote on the paper, folded it up and handed it to the woman, gesturing that she should give it to Ned with his coffee. Then she thanked the woman again, left the money for Ned's drink on the counter and left.

10

Ned sat up and stretched. It had been a more productive morning than he'd expected. He picked up the fresh cup of coffee that he didn't remember ordering and took a sip. And then he noticed that on the table next to it was a note addressed to him. Ned, it said simply on the front of the folded sheet.

He opened it and smiled. It was from Anna.

Hey Ned, didn't want to disturb you when you were on a roll. Here's my number if you fancy meeting for a coffee sometime. Anna

It was refreshing to meet someone who thought about someone other than themselves. Not many people who spotted him out in public would have thought to leave him be, that it might not be a good time to approach him. He loved that Anna had. It meant a lot to him. Made him feel as if she really did understand him and was in sharp contrast to other people in his life.

He had expected that leaving the country for a few months would mean that people understood that he wanted to get away from everything. He'd told everyone who needed to know, leaving things by saying that he'd see them when he got back and for the most part, people had accepted it. Freddie kept in touch pretty regularly but that was different because they were best friends. He'd exchanged a few FaceTime calls with his parents who lived in Tenerife but the main problem that was starting to manifest was Jeannie.

They'd got together fairly regularly over the past few years, but he was pretty sure she dated other people and that theirs was a relationship of convenience but now that he was taking some time away for the first time since they'd known each other, she was becoming increasingly needy. He had batted away a couple of texts she'd sent when he first left but in the last text she'd sent the night before, she'd been on about coming to visit him. He hadn't told anyone where he was going, apart from Freddie, and thank god because the last thing he wanted was her rocking up on his doorstep.

He pulled on his coat and hat and thanked Sigríður, as well as attempting to say, 'see you tomorrow,' in Icelandic. She gave him a wide grin and said something in Icelandic that he assumed was about the note since she was miming writing at the same time. He nodded and grinned, even though he had no idea what he was affirming.

Should he call Anna? He did want to see her. She was refreshing and made him feel grounded and safe. It was strange. But was it the right time to get into anything like that? Then again, did it have to be a relationship? Not ringing someone because he assumed that was going to be the result was ridiculous. He would call her.

He walked back to his apartment and spent the rest of the day working on melodies to go with the lyrics that had poured out of him that morning. It felt amazing to be productive again and it felt right. Although he was spending a lot of time on it, it didn't feel like an effort because he was enjoying it and that was how he knew it was good. Or at least, he hoped it was. In these moments when it was going well, he was riding on the crest of the biggest wave in the world. But there were moments of doubt, of course there were.

By mid-afternoon he'd come to a natural stop and opened the fridge to get a beer, thinking that now would be a good time to call Anna. He settled in the chair next to the window and rummaged in his pocket for the note from her when his phone sprang into life with a FaceTime call from Freddie.

'Neddy boy! How's it going?' Freddie was in his studio with a beer in his hand as well.

'Good timing, mate.' Ned waved his beer at the camera. 'Yeah, it's been a good day. I've got a new song down. I'm pretty pleased with it.'

'Ready to share yet?'

'God, no.'

Freddie laughed. 'You know where I am when it is.'

Ned loved his friend's support but knew that even if he wrote the worst song in the world, Fred would say it was brilliant.

'I'll bear it in mind, thanks. So is the honeymoon over yet?'

'We're back in the studio this week, it's a little on the anti-social side for Sophia, so yeah. Back to reality.'

'And how's the new material shaping up?'

'Ah, you know, same old, same old. It's what people want so it's all good.' Freddie paused. 'But it's not the same without you.'

'Writing alone isn't the same either. I feel like a bloody hermit.'

'I thought you'd made a friend. Didn't you go to that gig last night?'

'Yeah. They played one of our songs and I had to leave.'

'That bad was it?'

It was easy to laugh about it now. 'They were doing okay, it was just weird. Took me right back.'

'I get that, Ned. You've taken yourself out of it and then that pulls you right back in.'

'No one knows who I am here, and I like that. It's the first time I've felt like I can be myself for years. Last night when they started playing that song, I thought straight away that everyone would turn around and stare at me. I mean, obviously they didn't.'

'Really? No one knows?'

'Okay, you won't believe this but that woman who was at your wedding, the one I spoke to at the church. She's here.'

'She's stalking you?'

'No, it's a coincidence.'

Freddie made a face. 'Is it?'

'If anything, she's like the total opposite of a fan. It's like she sees me, or something. Not Ned Nokes from The Rush.'

'That's cool. So, you have someone to hang out with.'

'Maybe. She gave me her number.'

'And you've called her?'

'Not yet. But I think I will.'

'The reason I called... Jeannie's been asking around for you.'

Ned sighed. 'I told her I was away for three months. But yeah, she's been texting me.'

'She's been asking everyone to see if anyone knows where you are. Don't worry, me and the lads haven't said anything, and you know we won't. I just thought you might want to try and nip it in the bud, whatever it is.'

'I don't know what she wants. I don't really know what to say to her.'

'Maybe just tell her that whatever you had is over?'

'But it wasn't anything, you know that.'

'I know, Ned. But you don't want a disgruntled woman on your tail. Especially not now when everything else is so good.'

'Okay. Thanks for the heads up, Fred.'

'I'll let you get on. Remember I want to be the first to hear the new stuff!'

Despite feeling that Jeannie had no reason to think that he owed her anything, Ned felt obliged to deal with whatever her issue was before he embarked on whatever he might be starting with Anna. He honestly didn't think he had anything to apologise for with Jeannie but equally, Freddie's words rang in his ears, and he did want to nip whatever it was in the bud. Having a fan base made him all too aware that people could read more into situations or relationships than he'd intended. It was something he'd always taken pains to avoid and that was why being with Jeannie sometimes had seemed like the safer option. But apparently not.

He finished his beer and called her before he could change his mind.

'Hi.'

'Ned, it's so great to hear from you.'

He immediately regretted calling. He could hear in her voice that she was too pleased to hear from him.

'I just wanted to get in touch… to make sure we're on the same page.'

'Yes, great. So, I was thinking as it's been a few weeks, I'd love to come and visit you.'

'Look, Jeannie. I know we've had a good time in the past but it's not… it's not a relationship. Not for me.'

There was silence. Ned wasn't sure whether she'd hung up on him but there was no tone to indicate that the call had ended.

'Yes, I realise it wasn't a relationship, technically.' She sounded defensive but what had he expected? 'I just thought you being away was no reason to put a stop to things.'

'The thing is, I guess now that I've left the band, I'm in a different place. Not just… literally.'

'I'm not an idiot, Ned. I just didn't realise that you leaving the band meant your whole life was going to change. But fine. If that's how it is, that's fine.'

It wasn't fine and he wished she'd taken it better but as she hadn't, he was going to have to roll with it because the only other option was giving in and saying he'd see her again. And he didn't want that, especially now that he'd seen this side of her.

'I am sorry, Jeannie.'

'Me too.'

'Take care,' he said before hanging up.

He exhaled, feeling at the same time bad, for having upset Jeannie but also that a weight he'd never realised he was carrying, had lifted. He headed to the fridge for another beer and wondered whether to call Anna. As much as he wanted to, he felt like the spectre of Jeannie would think it was too soon. He laughed at himself but decided that tomorrow would do just as well. Best not to seem too keen. Better to call tomorrow, a bit like a fresh start.

11

The following day, Jonas was working in the office so Anna didn't get her usual early morning wake-up call. She'd decided that if she woke up naturally before six-thirty she'd head to the bakery, even if she hadn't heard from Ned by then. It could be that he was still in the writing zone he'd been in yesterday and if that was the case it'd be reassuring to see it because waiting for him to call was absolute torture.

As it was, she didn't wake up until Rachel came and sat on her bed with a cup of tea for each of them at around nine o'clock.

'I thought I might drive round one of my tour routes today if you fancy it?'

'Thanks for the tea. That sounds good. I need the distraction.'

'No contact?'

'Nothing.'

'You sound remarkably like you're interested in him.'

'I'm starting to think that's true.'

It was a chilly but gloriously sunny day. Rachel had borrowed Jonas's jeep and they were heading through the wilderness to visit someone who dyed wool using plants and other natural dyes. Anna wasn't sure it sounded like the flagship tour destination Rachel thought it was but she didn't want to put a damper on the day.

'We're going past a really cool waterfall so we'll stop there because I think my guests would enjoy that and it's not on any other tour company's itinerary.'

'Great.'

'Come on Anna, more enthusiasm, please. This is the inaugural tour for Icelandic Craft Adventures, and you have me all to yourself.'

'Sorry.'

'It's because he hasn't called, isn't it?'

'Ever since I met him at Freddie's wedding… '

'You fancied him then, I know you did. It's not like you, I've never known you moon around like this over a man. It's a sign.'

'I'm not mooning,' said Anna, laughing at Rachel's turn of phrase. 'Because I'm not a teenager.'

'Correct me if I'm wrong, but in the whole time I've known you, you've never had anything other than a brief dalliance with anyone and even if a brief thing turns into something more, it's no more than a regular booty call.'

'Rach!'

'Am I wrong?'

Her friend took her eyes off the road to momentarily fix her with a look that said she wanted to hear the truth.

'You're not wrong.'

Anna gazed out of the window at the barren landscape which was whipping past them, with the odd puff of steam coming randomly from the earth.

'Something happened. I don't know how to explain it, but I instantly felt something for him. It's ridiculous.'

'No, it's normal, Anna. That is what happens when you're attracted to someone.'

'Someone I don't know. Someone who I've had a couple of

conversations with in my life and someone who now has my number and hasn't called me.' The almost tangible memory of dancing with him was all that was keeping her from thinking that she had imagined the whole thing.

'Someone who trusted you the other night to help him out when he was vulnerable and had no one to turn to.'

'I might have foisted myself on him, to be fair.'

'Either way, I saw how he looked at you that night and it was different to how he was looking at any of us, believe me. Just give him time. He obviously came here to get away. It might not feel that straightforward to him to behave like a normal person.'

Anna raised her eyebrows and smiled.

'I know about the psyche of celebrities,' said Rachel defensively, but she grinned.

'Good, because I don't know about anyone's psyche, least of all my own.'

'You'll be fine. You just need to learn to give in to your feelings a bit more. I mean, when was the last time you did something for fun? Not work-related.'

Anna cast her mind back over the past few months. Work had been so busy.

'Just because it's work-related, it doesn't mean it isn't fun.'

'Okay, let me put it another way. What outside of work makes you happy.'

The tentative tone of Rachel's question wasn't lost on Anna. She wouldn't say she was a particularly happy person. She was too calculated and didn't let herself go very often.

'I see what you're trying to do. No, I'm not the happiest person on the planet but that's just me, Rach. You know me, that's what I've always been like.'

'And I'm not saying that you need a man to make you happy. I know it seems like that's what happened for me with Jonas, but it was coming here that made me realise what I wanted, not him. That was just serendipity.'

'Sorry, just to be clear, that has not happened to me since I've been here. I'm never going to find my happy place somewhere that forces you to evaluate your clothing for survival reasons rather than fashion every time you leave the house. I don't even know what fashion is anymore.'

'Oh god, Anna. I've missed you.'

They pulled into a clear area off the side of the road that Rachel referred to as a car park, but which had nothing to indicate that other than that it was marginally flatter than the rest of the land around them.

'Okay, here we are. This is Faxi waterfall.'

Rachel parked the car and they both pulled on their hats and gloves before walking the short distance to the waterfall. Outside the city, it felt a lot colder and for once, Anna was glad of the knitwear she'd borrowed from Rachel. As well as the hats she'd knitted, she'd knitted a jumper and lent it to Anna. It was just as scratchy as the hat but with layers underneath it, she didn't notice. She had said she'd start knitting one for Anna which had sounded like a threat at the time, but now Anna realised that it was a generous offer.

The waterfall was impressive, not because of its height which was about 7 metres, but because of its width and the unbelievable blueness of the water.

'What do you think?' said Rachel. 'Isn't it lovely?'

Anna was surprised at how close she could get to the water. There was nothing to stop you from jumping or falling in anywhere which seemed unusual to her.

'It's pretty amazing, actually.' She smiled, enjoying her first taste of an Iceland other than Reykjavik. 'So, this is the kind of thing you did with Jonas? How he won you over?'

'Mmm. It's so different to anything I'd ever seen before and it's right here on our doorstep, I mean, it's incredible.'

Anna understood the concept of amazing natural wonders,

but she didn't feel any kind of affinity with them that meant she'd want to visit them any more often than she had throughout her life so far, which was next to never.

'And there's a restaurant over there by the looks of it,' Anna said, thinking that a coffee would be just the thing to warm her up. 'Do you think that counts as research?'

'Definitely. And I have it on good authority that the fish and chips are top-notch.'

'It's barely lunchtime, Rach.'

'You're on holiday. You're not tied to schedules.'

They walked around to view the waterfall from higher up before Anna pointed out that she hadn't signed up for a hike and they headed for the restaurant. Just as they were heading inside, Anna's phone rang. It was an unknown number and her heart leapt uncharacteristically as the thought that it could be Ned engulfed her.

'Answer it,' said Rachel, putting a calming hand on Anna's arm. 'I'll wait inside.'

'Hello?'

'Anna, hi, it's Ned.'

'Oh, hi. How are you?'

'Yes, good thanks. Look, I wanted to say thanks for the coffee yesterday.'

'No problem. You looked like you were in for the long haul.'

'I guess I was.'

He paused and she waited, feeling that having waited a whole day to call her, he'd better have something to say.

'I was hoping I might have seen you this morning.'

Managing to stop herself from squealing with joy, she said, 'Early mornings aren't my natural habitat. It just didn't happen today.'

He laughed and Anna grinned.

'So maybe the other end of the day is a better time to catch you?'

Anytime would be fine, she wanted to say. She'd happily get up as early as anything if he was suggesting it. 'Coffee's not great in the evening though.'

'I'll see your coffee and raise you a lunch. Tomorrow?'

'Great.'

'I'll text you the plan,' he said and then rang off.

'Hello?' Anna said quietly into the phone just to make sure he had hung up, then she hugged it to her chest, put it in her pocket and went inside to find Rachel. It was the first solid sign she had that he liked her. They'd slow-danced and held hands on the back of his minor meltdown but maybe that would have happened anyway, it was just the moments they'd found themselves in. This was different. It was a date.

'I can tell by your face that it was him,' said Rachel, handing a menu to Anna as she sat down. 'I'm having the fish and chips.'

Anna put the menu down without looking at it.

'He wants to go out for lunch tomorrow.'

'That's a date, then,' said Rachel, her eyes bright.

'It looks like it. I mean, it's not coffee which is what I suggested.'

'It's good, Anna. You like him and he likes you back.'

'Yes,'

Rachel frowned. 'What is it? You looked like the Cheshire Cat when you came in and now you look like you think you've made a mistake.'

'I don't want it to be a mistake but we're both on holiday for want of a better word. What happens when we go home? Best case scenario, we like each other. What then?' Because they were from completely different worlds. She was basically a fixer who worked for people like him. Someone who helped to construct and maintain the carefully designed facade that existed around celebrities. It could be strange being friends with someone who was on the other side of that. And if they ended up more than friends... well that might be even harder to navigate.

'Don't sabotage it before you've even been on the first date,' Rachel said firmly. 'You deserve this. Grab it with both hands and just let yourself go for once.'

It was what she needed to hear and what she'd missed about having Rachel around. They were both great at sorting out each other's lives, at seeing what was what from a distance.

The visit to the dyer, Agnes, which Anna had expected to be pretty dull was surprisingly interesting and gave Anna a feel for what Rachel was offering. As a non-arty-crafty person, she could appreciate that someone who was would be in their element and the additional sight-seeing that Rachel was planning to combine with it would make for a really enjoyable day out because that's exactly what Anna had had.

Rachel had been very taken with the wool. It was a different colour palette from the usual Icelandic wool that was sold everywhere. The colours that Agnes created which came from the flora and fauna were soft and heathery. She had bunches of dried plants hanging from the rafters in her studio which was heated very effectively by a huge wood-burning stove in the corner, and she used these to create her dyes.

She took them outside to see the wool she was dying at the moment using foraged berries. Agnes had to use whatever was plentiful at the time of year and with almost all of the flowers over, berries were her current dye of choice. She stirred the dye bath and hooked out a skein of wool to show them, which was a rich pinky plum colour.

Rachel purchased enough wool to knit a jumper for herself, suggesting to Anna that it was necessary to try the product that she was essentially recommending by taking her clients there and then they set off back to Reykjavik.

On the way back Anna found herself taking more notice of the landscape. There were pockets of green that she hadn't noticed before and she thought that Agnes probably had just as much fun collecting her dyes as she did using them.

For the first time, she could understand the affinity that Rachel had for the place. There was so much more to it than what she'd seen in Reykjavik, and she was beginning to understand how Jonas had helped her see this slightly magical side to the country.

'Thanks for today, Rach. I completely get what you're trying to do now, more than I did before. We need to get that feeling across to people. Make them feel like they're part of something special, something they wouldn't normally see coming here as a tourist.'

'That's it, exactly,' she said, her eyes glinting with excitement as she took her eyes off the road momentarily to smile at Anna. 'I knew you'd get it.'

'I think what you've done so far is great, but it doesn't convey the uniqueness of what you're offering. It's not just a craft tour, Rach. I mean, Agnes, that's her life. She's foraging for her raw materials and turning the fruit of the land into something unique and beautiful. That's what we need to sell.'

'In the same way that it's a unique opportunity for tourists to see the natural wonders, these craft people are natural wonders in a different way.'

'We just need to think of a better way to say that, Rach. Then you've nailed it.'

12

Inviting Anna to lunch was the easy part. Where was he going to take her? He was struggling with the fact that before he'd left the band, he'd have felt the need to go somewhere swanky to impress her. Somewhere that she would find breathtaking and somewhere so expensive that she would think he was amazing.

But he didn't think that kind of thing would impress Anna. He didn't know much about her, but he did know that she treated him like anyone else. To her, he didn't think he was Ned Nokes from The Rush, and he didn't feel the need to show her what he could do with his money. Besides, he didn't feel like that Ned Nokes anymore. He was beginning to discover the person that he actually was now that he'd left all the other crap behind, giving himself the time and space to get to know himself for the first time in his adult life. So why pretend to be that guy who could flash his money around and pay for whatever he wanted? That wasn't the guy that Anna knew.

It also didn't change the fact that he had no idea where to go. After some random googling which turned up nothing out of the ordinary, he decided to trust a local with his problem and rang Brun.

'Hey Brun, I'm wondering if you can help me out. I'm looking for somewhere to take someone for lunch. Somewhere that's not for tourists, authentic. And a good atmosphere.'

'Ah, is it a date?'

'Sort of.' It was a date as far as Ned was concerned and he hoped Anna was thinking along the same lines. But he had already gathered that theirs was a tight-knit friendship group, and he didn't want any of his assumptions to be relayed back to Anna, so it seemed safer to play it cool.

'I like Sjavargrillid, they do a lobster taco that is *furðulegur.* It is all seafood but fresh and delicious.'

'That sounds great, thanks. Going to any more gigs?'

'Not for a week or so. I am on the rota for Northern Lights excursions and the aurora is good at the moment. No nights off for me for a while.'

They arranged to meet for a drink the following week, then Ned called the restaurant and made a reservation, crossing his fingers that Anna liked seafood.

He texted her to say that he'd meet her on the road where they'd parted ways the other night, at one o'clock. She responded straight away with a thumbs-up emoji.

Happy to take Brun's word for it that it was a good place, Ned still wanted to know where it was, so he knew how to get there and didn't look stupid in front of Anna. He'd had a productive morning of writing, but it wasn't flowing enough for him to feel he wanted to spend the rest of the day fiddling around with melodies and lyrics. Instead, he pulled his coat on and went for an exploratory stroll.

Once he'd clocked the restaurant which looked like it would be perfect with its dimly lit, wooden-clad interior and intimate tables for two along one side of the room, he carried on strolling back towards the harbour, thinking that it might be nice to see the Northern Lights while he was here. He'd never seen them before, and it hadn't occurred to him to look into anything like that which seemed like a missed opportunity now that he thought about it. In fact, he was missing a lot of things that were right under his nose. Right now, he was standing outside the Harpa, a concert hall perched right on the edge of the harbour. He'd seen it from his apartment and been mesmerised by the way the front of it was lit up to look like the Northern Lights, yet he'd never ventured inside.

The sheer size of the interior was incredible and filled with light from the strange structure of honeycomb windows that covered the whole building. Ned headed to the cafe near the entrance and bought himself a coffee, taking a minute to peruse the stand full of brochures advertising everything from tours to restaurants to swimming pools. He picked up a small brochure claiming to be the ultimate guide to Reykjavik nightlife and walked up the majestic staircase to where he'd spotted a sofa.

As he flicked through, he came to a list of music venues and discovered that there was an open mic night every week at a bar very close to where he was now. He loved the idea of sharing his music in that kind of way. Maybe it was too soon, but he felt like he had a couple of decent songs, and it might be a good opportunity to get a feel for how his music might be received while he was still able to be anonymous.

Once he'd finished his coffee, he decided to find the bar and scope it out to see if it was somewhere he thought he'd feel comfortable playing.

Given that it was mid-afternoon on a weekday, the place was almost deserted, so the barman greeted Ned as soon as he walked in.

'I'll have a beer, please.'

'Coming right up.'

'What's the crowd like for your open mic night?' asked

Ned, as he arranged his beer so that it was perfectly centred on a beermat.

'Yes, it is popular. There are some regular musicians, but anyone is welcome.'

'All kinds of music?'

'Oh, yes. All kinds. People are very supportive.'

'That's good to know. *Takk.*'

'Are you thinking of playing?'

'Maybe. I might come along and have a look first.'

'You are very welcome. If you want to play, come early to get on the list.'

'Okay, thanks.'

Ned picked up his beer and went to sit at a table next to the windows that looked out over the water. He smiled to himself, finding it funny that he was even contemplating putting himself out there, sharing the music he was proud of with no plan or agenda or anyone to please except himself.

The following day, he walked to the place where he'd arranged to meet Anna. He was five minutes early, but she came down the cobbled path from her house only a minute or so after he'd got there.

'Hey, you look great,' he said, before kissing her on the cheek. It felt natural, something he would do with a friend, and he hoped that's what she was. It was hard to see what she was wearing under her coat, but her hair was in soft, more styled waves than it'd been before, and she was hatless which looked more glamorous straight away.

'You look great too,' she said, with an appreciative smile.

He'd made more effort to get ready today than he had at any time since Freddie's wedding. He'd used some of the hair product that had been languishing in his toiletry bag to tame the lazy curls at the front of his hair into something resembling an intentional hairstyle and he'd decided to wear a shirt. He had a long-sleeved t-shirt underneath — he wasn't ignoring the fact that it got a little bit colder here every day that headed closer to October, but he wanted Anna to see that he'd made an effort.

They walked alongside each other through the old town towards the bottom of the street that led to Hallsgrimkirka, the landmark cathedral.

'Where are we going?' Anna asked him.

'We're going for seafood. Is that okay?' If she had a seafood allergy or was a vegetarian, his careful plans would be ruined.

'I love seafood,' she said, tucking her arm into his. 'I had some amazing fish and chips yesterday, right next to a waterfall.'

'Wow, that sounds cool. And adventurous.'

'My friend Rachel is with Jonas who owns Iceland Adventures, so I suppose it was inevitable that I'd end up doing something like that. But I enjoyed it more than I thought I would.'

'Brun was saying that the Northern Lights are pretty reliable at the moment. Have you seen then yet?'

'No. Jonas says it's rare to see them from here because of the light pollution. Have you?'

'I haven't but I'd like to.'

He looked at Anna and she had the same expression on her face that he imagined was on his. Without saying anything, they had just decided to see the Northern Lights together.

'Here we are,' he said, holding the door open for her and loving the way she looked at him from underneath her lashes as she thanked him.

'I hear the lobster tacos are amazing,' said Ned as they were shown to their table and began looking at the menu.

'I love lobster. I think that's me sorted.'

'Should we order a bottle of wine?'

She nodded. 'You choose.'

'I think I might ask for a recommendation of something that pairs well with lobster,' he said, closing his menu.

Anna began telling him about her friend Rachel's new business. He enjoyed watching her talk. She was animated and enthusiastic as she spoke, but he wanted to hear about her.

'So, I assume you live in London?'

'Mmm, I have a flat in Soho.'

'Really? That's cool.'

'It is in an amazing location, but the stairs are a killer, and the windows are open even when they're closed, if you know what I mean.'

He laughed. 'I've lived in places like that.'

'Really,' she said, giving him a doubtful look.

'Yes.' He grinned and nodded. 'Before the band took off, I was doing session work, the pay's not amazing but you need to be in central London so you take what you can get.'

'I like my place. It's better than sharing so I don't mind that it's a bit... tired.'

'And what do you do? I know you were working at Freddie's wedding but there were a lot of people doing a lot of different things at that wedding.'

He saw something in her eyes before she blinked it away and said, 'I was helping with the photoshoot.'

Oh, right. I guess that's why you took charge when that drone thing happened. Well, you handled it like a pro.'

'Thanks. It was a great wedding, I felt so bad that happened to spoil it.'

'No, they had an amazing day, and it gives them something to remember it by, doesn't it?'

'I guess so.'

Their wine arrived and then their food. He'd also ordered the lobster tacos and they were fantastic. They barely spoke until they'd both finished eating and then sat, sipping on the wine, chatting easily.

'How's your writing going?'

'Good, I think. It's different. Not for me but from what people will expect from me.'

'It's good that you're not worried about that. You should write what you want, it has to be authentic. Then people will love it anyway.'

'I hope so.' He took a breath and decided to share his plan with her. 'I'm thinking of trying out a song or two at an open mic night.'

'Oh, wow, that's a great idea!'

'Really? You don't think it's weird?'

'I don't think it's weird. Obviously, I can't vouch for whether you're any good or not.'

He laughed. 'Maybe I could try it out on you first?'

'I'd love that,' she said, looking at him with those eyes that told him the things she hadn't said.

'Now?'

'Now's great.'

13

Ned's apartment gave Anna a whole different perspective on Reykjavik, seeing the city for the first time from above rather than from within the maze of shops and tiny houses that made up the old part of the town. She stood at the window trying to see if she could spot Rachel and Jonas's house, but she didn't know the place well enough to get her bearings and couldn't pick out their tiny house from all the other coloured roofs.

'It's a great view,' she said to Ned as he made them both a cup of tea. He'd offered more wine, but it was still early, and Anna didn't want to feel any woozier than she already did.

Ned handed her a mug of steaming tea that was just the right colour. 'It's my favourite place to sit. I love watching the harbour.'

Anna sat down in his favourite chair next to the window. 'Mmm. I bet you get nothing done sat here.'

'It's nice to have something to look at while I'm messing around with melodies,' he said, going over to sit on the sofa.

Anna twirled the chair to face him and sipped her tea. He looked more relaxed than she felt. He'd put his tea down on the table that separated them and was sat back with one arm resting along the back of the sofa. He'd taken his boots off when they'd come in and was wearing brightly striped socks.

He took a sip of his tea and then reached behind the sofa and grabbed a guitar, pulling it onto his lap and strumming a couple of chords. His hair began to flop down over his forehead as he looked down and Anna felt her stomach clench in an unfamiliar way. Much the same as it had when she'd been stood in the church porch with him.

'Let's hear it then,' she said, smiling in what she hoped was an encouraging way.

'Give me a sec,' he said. He put the guitar down on the sofa and disappeared back into the hallway, coming back a few seconds later with his notebook in his hand. 'I don't know the lyrics yet. And I might think of something better anyway.'

He positioned himself on the sofa again with the guitar, looked up at Anna with a shy smile and began.

As soon as he began singing, Anna melted. She found herself listening to every word he sang with a feeling of elation and at the same time sadness that each word was taking her towards the end of this incredible experience.

It could have been because no one had ever played for her like that; it felt intimate as if Ned were giving something of himself to her in that moment. It could have been the lyrics, which she loved and that told the story of a man who sees a beautiful woman on a beach in a storm and something magical about the waves becoming part of her and her hair being wavy. Whatever the reason, it gave Anna a sense of a magical fairy-tale and even though it was impossible, she felt as if the song was about her.

Before he had finished playing, she went over and sat next to him. As he played, he turned to face her, no longer looking at the words that were scribbled in the notebook but instead looking right into her eyes, with his soulful brown ones. There was suddenly an overwhelming connection between them and as Ned played the last few notes, Anna closed her eyes, savouring the feeling.

'What did you think?' he asked softly, as he laid the guitar down next to him.

'I think you'll win anyone over with that song, Ned. It was... amazing. I loved it, it's like nothing I've ever heard before.'

He leaned towards her. 'You could be that girl...'

His fingers touched hers and it was like electricity shooting through her. She could see in his eyes that he'd felt it too. She knew what was going to happen next as if it were written in the stars. Their lips met, after what seemed like an eternity of moving towards each other. They were both holding back; there was nothing urgent about it. Not because it wasn't what they both wanted but because it was the beginning of something. Something to be mindful of because of what it meant.

Anna had never felt so in sync with anyone before. Nothing like this had ever happened to her before and she knew that nothing ever would again. How had she found this man who had awoken these feelings in her?

Ned's fingers found her cheek and he slowly moved his fingers to the nape of her neck as their kisses become more intense, gently urging her towards him. In turn, she pulled his t-shirt out of his jeans and ran her hands around his waist, making him groan with pleasure.

'Anna, what are you doing to me?' he murmured, letting her know that they were both on the same wavelength.

They lay in each other's arms in Ned's enormous bed looking out over the lights of the harbour that twinkled in the early evening dusk.

'I hope that song doesn't affect every woman like that,' said Ned.

'So do I. That feels like my song now.'

'Fair enough. I think anyone who appreciates my music as much as that deserves it to be gifted to them for all eternity.'

Anna snuggled into his side, unable to believe that she was in bed with him. Someone she thought she knew but who she now realised, no one knew.

'That is not what I was expecting to happen this afternoon,' she said.

'Mmm, me either. I can safely say that it ranks as one of the better afternoons I've had.'

'So unexpected.'

He kissed her forehead. 'Most of the best things in life are.'

Anna lazily traced her finger around his chest. 'Do you have any other songs?'

'I have lots of songs but since I came here, I've found something different. That song I played you, that's my best one but I've got a couple of others that are good, I think.'

'You should do the open mic night. You'll kill it.'

'It's tonight. I wasn't planning to play tonight but do you want to go out for food and then we could check it out?'

'Yes, that'd be great. Not yet though.'

'Of course, not yet.'

Later that evening, Anna took Ned to the Noodle Bar. Rachel had been insisting that she had to go there so as Ned had chosen the lunch venue, Anna suggested that for dinner as she knew nowhere else.

'Are you sure? It looks a bit dodgy,' said Ned as they approached.

Anna couldn't help but agree with his assessment but also wanted to be able to tell Rachel that she'd tried her recommendation.

'It's meant to be amazing. Come on, Rachel and Jonas come here all the time.'

Ned rolled his eyes but allowed himself to be dragged

inside where they both ordered the noodle broth with meat and all the trimmings.

'Okay, they're right. It's pretty good. On the spicy side but, yeah, delicious.'

They sat on bar stools at a counter in the window and chatted as they ate. Anna couldn't remember the last time she'd felt this relaxed with a man she'd been out with. Lunch had been okay too, although they had both been a bit nervous, but now, it was as if they'd been together for ages.

'What's your favourite kind of food?' she asked Ned.

'Hmm, that's a hard question. If you're in another country, the local food can be amazing. I love Korean street food, it's insane. I guess Mexican is my all-time favourite though.'

'I love a Taco Bell burrito.'

Ned laughed. 'Me too. One is never enough, although I'm not sure that counts as Mexican food.'

The open mic night was well underway by the time they got to the bar, but they managed to find a couple of seats at the back. Ned went to the bar and got beers and then they settled in to listen.

'It's a good turnout,' Anna said between acts.

'I don't know if that's good for me or bad,' said Ned with a grimace.

'It's good because they'll love you. Isn't that the whole point of this kind of thing? To get your music out there to people?' Anna wasn't sure whether Ned would have that same motivation. Surely, he could get a record deal from anyone, with his background and contacts in the music world.

Ned nodded. 'Maybe next week. Gives me something to work towards.'

Anna reached over and squeezed his hand. 'I'm looking forward to the next preview.'

He grinned at her and slid his fingers between hers, their

hands resting on his thigh, as the next song started.

The next time Ned went to get a drink, Anna texted Rachel to let her know she might not be back tonight. Just in case. It felt a bit presumptuous, but Anna felt she had good reason to think she might be invited to stay over, and she couldn't think of anything nicer than waking up to Ned in the morning.

'No worries, enjoy yourself!' Rachel replied, with a heart-eyes emoji and a kissing-heart emoji.

They stayed until the very end partly because the music was brilliant but partly, for Anna at least, because she wanted the night to last as long as possible.

The bar wasn't far from Ned's apartment, but he didn't head that way when they left. They were holding hands and Anna wasn't particularly paying attention to where they were going. She kept glancing across at him, marvelling at what had happened between them in such a short space of time. By the time she noticed where they were, she knew that a night with him wasn't on the cards. She tried to ignore the sinking feeling of disappointment which was rapidly bringing her mood from ecstatic back to a more normal level.

He paused on Laugavegur, near the Snug shop and turned to face her, taking both of her hands in his.

'Anna, I've had the best day with you.'

The disappointment gave way to a fleeting feeling closer to the way she'd been feeling since lunchtime, and she smiled at him.

'Me too, Ned.'

'This is something different for me. I want you but at the same time I want to know how it feels not to be with you.' He looked up at the stars as he said, 'does that make any sense?'

If it hadn't been for listening to his song and having that exquisite feeling of wanting more but at the same time wanting it to never end, she might not have been able to

92

understand. But somehow, it made complete sense. And if she didn't feel the same way, if she wanted nothing more than to be with him every single second for the rest of time, she wasn't going to say that to him. Not tonight.

'It does make sense. There's no hurry, Ned. At all.'

He kissed her on the lips, a slow and lingering kiss that made her wish she'd insisted on spending the night together after all.

'Thank you.'

'Maybe catch up soon?' He had just told her he wanted space, to take it slow so as much as it pained her, she needed to play it cool.

'Tomorrow? I'll call you.'

She grinned. 'Great. Night, Ned.'

'Night, Anna. Sleep tight.'

She made her way along the road to where the street turned up towards the cobbled path, then turned and watched Ned walking away. He had his hands in his pockets now and then he stopped, ran his hands through his hair and punched the air with both hands, then carried on walking.

Anna felt like she was going to burst with happiness. She'd never felt like this before. It was incredible. Something she thought she'd never find, had stopped looking for even, had found her. In Iceland of all places. Maybe Rachel was right, and this place was magical after all.

14

The next day, although she was still on a high, Anna was determined not to sit around waiting for Ned to call. This time, she felt sure he would so there was no need to be in a state of nervous anticipation. But it was hard. From the moment she woke, every minute that he hadn't called or texted felt like an hour. She needed a distraction.

She pulled her laptop out of her bag for the first time since she'd arrived in Reykjavik, probably the longest time she hadn't laid her fingers on a keyboard for years. She smiled because she never would have believed it would be possible, but she had managed to leave her life behind and was actually beginning to relax. Especially after yesterday.

Rachel was upstairs starting to pack up ready for the move and had implored Anna not to speak to her. Packing was boring and everything was a distraction. She'd rashly told Jonas that she was happy to do all the packing since she was working less than him at the moment and had regretted it the instant his face lit up in happy agreement.

Anna decided she was going to do a bit of a PR plan for Rachel. She began by searching the internet for some top-end UK-based travel agents and tour operators so that she had a list of targets. Then she opened up the graphic design software she always used for social media posts at work and using Rachel's page from Jonas's website as a reference, she began crafting a pitch.

'Hey,' said Rachel, coming onto the kitchen looking dejected. 'Coffee?'

'Thanks. How's it going?'

'God, I thought the bedroom would be an easy win, especially because half of my clothes are still in storage, but Jonas has a surprising amount of clothes.'

'Really? He looks like he wears virtually the same thing day in and day out.'

'I know! But he has twenty black long-sleeved t-shirts, about twenty sets of base layers— '

'I'm going to stop you there, Rach. It's cold here, even in September. I bet in the middle of winter he wears ten of everything all at the same time.'

Rachel laughed, put the coffees on the table and sat down.

'I feel like sitting down is a distraction, Rach.'

She groaned and flopped her head dramatically onto the table.

'Look, finish your coffee, get back to it and I'll have a surprise for you.' She wanted to show her email to Rachel before she sent it just to make sure she was happy with it.

Rachel's eyes lit up. 'Is it something to do with Ned?'

'No, I already told you what happened yesterday.'

'I know but I'm desperate for the next instalment.'

'Rachel, you're moving in with the man of your dreams, or at least you will be if you can get the packing done, and you're getting married. You don't need my love story; you've got your own.'

'But it is a love story, right?' she asked Anna with wide eyes.

'I didn't mean to say that.' But that was what she hoped it was. She shot Rachel a wry smile.

'Say no more. Right, I've got my second wind.'

By the time Anna had the pitch email ready to go, she began to hear some shuffling and banging coming from upstairs and went to investigate.

Rachel was trying to manhandle a huge cardboard box down the ladder that led from the mezzanine.

'You should have called me!' Anna said, climbing up a few rungs so that she could grab the bottom of the box and help lower it down. 'Didn't Jonas say not to bring any boxes down?'

'I don't feel like I've accomplished anything if they're up here. I want him to see how much I've done.'

Between them they managed to bring all the boxes down, stacking them in the corner of the lounge. Anna ventured up the ladder to have a look at what had been achieved.

'Nice job, there's literally nothing left up here.'

'That's the idea. We're going to start taking some stuff over to the new house tonight. Do you want to come and see?'

'I'd love to!' Anna said, trying to ignore the thought that now she may end up turning Ned down if he called with a plan. But Rachel was her best friend and buying a house with Jonas was a huge deal.

'Great!'

'Come and look at what I've been doing.'

They sat at the kitchen table with a cup of tea each while Anna showed Rachel the email she'd designed. As well as being peppered with beautiful images of Iceland and some of the crafts and workshops, it told the brief story of how Rachel came to set up her tours. How she'd organised the design call for the Snug store to source stock from local artisans and how that had led to her living in Iceland and setting up her own tours. Then she'd told Agnes's story, okay, it was pure imagination, but the point was to entice people.

'Don't you think it's a bit boring, explaining what I did

before?'

'Definitely not. You have to sell the story, Rach. No offence but anyone could pick this up and organise the tours. The difference is the story, how you fell in love with Iceland and how you discovered these artisans and have brought their skills to the attention of a mainstream retailer in a way that doesn't damage their ideologies.'

'Wow. I mean, that sounds amazing, thank you so much.'

'I'm just telling your story, Rach. You did all the hard work; I'm just presenting the package.'

'So, who are you going to send that to?'

Anna showed Rachel the list, having already populated her email with their bcc'd email addresses.

'Good to go?'

'It feels like a big moment, for some reason. This takes it to another level.'

Anna nodded. 'But you can do it, Rach. You already have, you just need to tell people now.'

'Okay'

Rachel placed her finger on the trackpad and tapped.

'I feel like we should celebrate. And we've both worked hard this morning.'

'Fantastic idea.'

They headed out to a cocktail bar, Slippsbarrin, which boasted that it launched the concept of cocktails in Reykjavik and had great views of the harbour. It wasn't too far from where she'd been with Ned the night before. And not far from his apartment.

'It has to be a mojito,' Rachel said as they sat down, before they'd even looked at the menu.

'I can go along with that. I can't remember the last time I had a cocktail. It might even have been our last night out in London before you came here.'

'Really? At that bar off Seven Dials where the barman

fancied you.'

'And who can blame him?' said Anna, attempting to flick her tangled windblown hair over her shoulder and giving Rachel a sultry look. 'Anyway, I've been a rosé girl lately.'

'And I've been drinking beer. Jonas isn't that keen on cocktails.'

Once they'd got their drinks in their hands, they clinked glasses and said 'Cheers!'

It was like the old days, and they had a great time chatting about Rachel's business and the wedding plans. Anna's phone buzzed with a call.

'Hello?'

'Hey, Anna.' It was Ned. She'd been having such a nice time that she'd almost forgotten he'd said he would call. Almost.

'Hi.'

Rachel got up from her chair and gestured that she would get them more drinks and went to the bar.

'I've missed you today but on the other hand, it's been pretty productive.'

'Mine's been like that too.'

'Distraction?'

Did that mean it was the same for him, had he spent all day wishing he was with her?

'Yep. Otherwise, I'd have been sitting staring at my phone until now.' Anna cringed. That admission felt a bit too honest.

He laughed softly. 'I'm sorry,' he said, 'same for me but I'm enjoying the inspiration that yesterday gave me.'

'So about tonight,' Anna began, watching Rachel chat to the barman. 'I kind of have something on. Rachel and Jonas are moving, and we need to take some stuff round to their new place.'

'Oh. Could I help?'

Anna's heart soared.

'Yes, that'd be great if you don't mind. It's only a few boxes I think.'

'Okay. I'll come round to yours. Text me where and when.'

'Great. See you later then.'

'Bye, Anna.'

Rachel came back over to the table with fresh cocktails, all wide-eyed and wondering.

'He's coming to help move your stuff later.'

'Oh, god, Anna. Ned Nokes is going to see my house when it looks crap, with everything half-packed.'

'To be fair, Rach, nothing's packed yet. Anyway, he's not coming to look at your house, he's coming so he can hang out with me.'

Her grin couldn't have been wider. Ned had called her, and he was coming to hang out. He didn't care what they were doing, he was just joining in. Like a normal guy who wanted to be with his... girlfriend. Was that what she was now?

'Cheers, Anna. Here's to you finally finding a man who deserves you. We hope.'

'Cheers!'

Anna and Rachel made it home at about five o'clock. Jonas was home from work and was in the middle of some packing of his own. The kitchen cupboard of outdoor clothes was empty, with the contents laid carefully in piles all over the lounge while Jonas was diligently but quite slowly, packing it all into boxes.

'Oh my god, Jonas. What are you doing? Ned is coming over. We need to get this place tidied up.' Rachel began randomly throwing things into the closest box.

Jonas gave Anna a bemused look to which she smiled and shrugged.

'We've been out for a drink,' she said. 'Ned's coming over to help move some stuff.'

'I see.' Jonas smiled and began removing the things from the box that Rachel had thrown in there. 'Rachel, he is not going to care about the mess. We are moving. It is normal for it to be messy when you are packing.'

Rachel sat down on the sofa, on top of some jackets, and put her head in her hands. 'I know. I just wanted to make a good impression. For Anna.'

'Don't worry. He's very laid back, he's not going to care. Anyway, I bet we can get all this packed before he comes, I told him to get here at six.'

The three of them made quick work of packing the outdoor clothes, leaving Rachel and Anna time to freshen up before Ned knocked on the door.

'Hey, come in,' said Jonas, introducing himself since it was the first time they'd met outside of the bar and Jonas wasn't sure Ned would have got everyone's names.

'Thanks.' He came in, took his boots and coat off and accepted Jonas's offer of a beer.

When Anna and Rachel appeared from the kitchen, he was sitting on the sofa using the hem of his t-shirt to wipe the fog off his glasses. He looked more like the Ned she remembered from the wedding. When he saw Anna, he put his glasses back on and went straight over and kissed her. His eyes were sparkling, and Anna could tell that he felt the same way that she did.

'You look great,' he said, not looking at her at all but keeping his eyes on hers.

'Thanks, so do you.' He smelt great too. The same as Anna remembered from before. She just wanted to bury her face in his neck.

They sat next to each other on the sofa while Rachel and Jonas sat opposite, him on a big chair and Rachel perched half on the arm and half on his lap.

'Where's your new place?'

'It is not far from here, maybe a ten-minute walk but we will take the jeep so that we can move some boxes.'

'I don't think we'll all fit in with the boxes. Maybe you two could walk and meet us there?' Rachel said, not managing, in her tipsy state, to hide her glee at having engineered some alone time for Anna and Ned.

'Sure, that's fine,' said Ned, taking Anna's hand and squeezing it. 'Let's find it on Google maps and we're sorted.'

'Okay. Let's load the Jeep.'

15

Anna and Ned helped load as many boxes as they could fit into the Jeep and waved Rachel and Jonas off before they locked the door and headed towards the new house. Jonas had dropped a pin to Ned so they could follow a route on Ned's phone. They decided to walk along the seafront as far as possible before heading inland. It wasn't the most direct way, but by unspoken agreement, any extra time it took was a bonus.

They walked along the wide pavement that snaked along the seafront, holding hands and looking at each other as much as anything else.

'It's great to see you again,' Ned said, tucking his phone in his back pocket now that he was sure of the way, at least for a while.

'I feel like it was longer ago than yesterday.'

'Me too. But then I've been writing all day. Time flies when that's going well.'

'How many songs?'

'One pretty solid one and the beginnings of a couple of others. I had one of those rare moments when the words and melody came all at once and I just rode that wave for most of the day.'

He looked at her in such a way that she wasn't sure she would be able to stop herself from pinning him against the sea wall and kissing him.

She tore her eyes away. 'I did some publicity for Rachel while she was packing and then we went out for cocktails as a reward.'

'Good day all round then.'

'Better now.'

He shot her a sideways look and a smile that just about finished her off before he pulled his hand away so that he could check his phone.

'It's up here,' he said, pointing to the next turning on their right.

Once they were on the right road, it was easy to find the house with the Jeep parked in the driveway. The houses were still in the same style as the ones in the older part of town, but they were larger and had more space around them.

'Nice place,' said Ned, appreciatively as Anna knocked on the door.

Rachel opened it. 'Welcome! Come in!'

There was a hallway with a wide wooden staircase running up one side and an impressive storage solution underneath where shoes and coats could be neatly kept.

They followed Rachel into the lounge which was painted in a dark blue shade that went well with the dark wood parquet floor and made the large room feel cosy. There were two huge sofas facing each other with a low coffee table in between.

'Wow, this is gorgeous, Rach. It's like your place now but bigger.'

'That's what we liked about it too,' Rachel said, going over to Jonas and snuggling into his side.

'Ned, would you like beer or champagne?' Jonas went into the kitchen and came back waving a bottle of each.

'Beer would be great, thanks mate. Do you need a hand in with the boxes?'

'That is a good idea, before we get carried away.' Jonas set the bottles down on the coffee table.

'And you need to give Anna and Ned a lift back, remember? We're going to stay here tonight,' she added.

'No need for that, I can walk Anna home,' said Ned.

He and Jonas headed outside and began bringing the boxes in, stacking them in the hall.

'I bet he walks you straight to his place,' Rachel said, raising her eyebrow.

'I hope so. Are you opening the champagne?'

Anna followed Rachel into the kitchen where she took a couple of tumblers out of a cupboard.

'Sorry, we've bought a few extra things now that we have more space, but I haven't packed the champagne glasses yet.'

'That should have been the first thing you packed but it'll taste fine in these lovely glasses.'

'They're from Snug.'

'I could have guessed. They have Snug written all over them.'

'It just makes me happy to have gorgeous things like these instead of plain boring ones.'

'I know. And that's why your house feels cosy and homely, and my flat doesn't.' Anna briefly wondered why she'd never made more of an effort to make her flat a bit more personal. 'I'm going to be more like that when I go home. I need to make my flat into more of a sanctuary rather than just somewhere to sleep.'

'Exactly. What's Ned's place like?'

'He's renting it, so I don't know that it's much of a reflection of his personality. I think he probably just came here with his guitar and not much else.'

'All done!' Jonas announced as they came back in. 'You

have started without us,' he said in mock outrage as he went into the kitchen for another bottle of beer while Ned sat on the sofa next to Anna and took his fogged-up glasses off again.

'This is becoming a bit of a problem now that it's getting colder outside,' he said, with a lopsided smile. He laid them down on the coffee table and picked up the beer that Jonas had opened for him.

'So, are you guys living here from now on or just staying tonight?' Anna asked.

'I think we'll stay here now. We only need the kitchen stuff and that's everything because we're going to leave the furniture for now. We've bought a new bed and the one at the other house will be for the spare room.'

'So, I've got my own place now?'

Rachel shrugged and looked at Jonas who nodded, 'I guess so.'

Once Anna and Rachel had finished the champagne between them, and Ned and Anna had had a tour of the house, they said goodnight and headed back into town.

'That's exciting for them, their first place together,' Ned said as they headed back towards the sea.

'It's so funny. It's like they've been together forever, they're so right for each other and it's only been a few months.'

'One of those relationships where they just knew.'

'But how often does that happen?' Anna said, realising as she said it that she was seriously beginning to think that was exactly what was happening to her.

'Perhaps more often than you think.' Ned squeezed her hand.

Anna looked across at him, but he was looking ahead as if he hadn't said something as profound as it sounded to her. Something she hoped he'd said because he thought that was happening to him.

He stopped and turned to face her, taking her hands in his.

'Would you like to stay with me tonight?'

She smiled and nodded. 'I'd love that.'

They walked back towards the harbour, towards Ned's place. Anna felt like she was walking on air the entire way. The prospect of a whole night with Ned was almost too much to bear. If he played that song to her again, she wasn't sure she'd make it to morning.

The wind that often blew cold from the sea was doing just that and by the time they reached Ned's they were both freezing. The temperature had dropped considerably since they'd set out earlier that evening with not enough layers on and neither of them had realised quite how cold it could get.

Ned pressed a button and a real-flame gas fire burst into life, immediately filling the place with a cosy vibe. He went to the bedroom and came back with the softest blanket in the world, handing it to Anna before going over to the kitchen.

'Hot chocolate with marshmallows?'

'Oh my god, yes, please. Have you got squirty cream as well?'

'Sadly not,' he grinned. 'You're lucky I have marshmallows, to be honest. They were in a welcome hamper, not from my own initiative.'

'That's okay. You're delivering the perfect drink for a night like this, it doesn't matter whether you bought the marshmallows or not.'

'The perfect drink… the pressure.' He grimaced and Anna laughed, snuggling herself further into the corner of the sofa underneath the blanket.

'It can't be the first time you've made a hot chocolate for someone,' Anna teased.

'You might be surprised.' He came over with the drinks, setting them down on the coffee table before sitting down next to Anna and tucking himself underneath the blanket as well.

'I think it's probably safe to say I've never made anything for anyone unless you count Freddie and the boys. My normal repertoire extends to opening bottles of champagne or beer and calling for a takeaway.'

'I feel especially honoured then,' said Anna, reaching for one of the mugs and nibbling a couple of the mini marshmallows off the top.'

'And you? Are you a seasoned hostess? In the food and drink sense,' he added quickly.

Anna laughed. 'No, not at all. Much the same as you, although I can make a mean mojito.'

'Nice skills.'

'I'm not the domestic type.'

'Neither am I. Until I left the band, I was hardly ever at home anyway. This place has given me a routine for the first time since I was a kid. Living the way I did before, I'm starting to see that it was highly overrated. I mean, I didn't want that anymore, that's why I left the band. I thought this would be just a break before I went back to all of that but on my own this time.'

'And now you're not sure?'

'I'm not. I love the music, but I guess I thought I'd go and find a big label who would take me for my name, not my music. That's not what I want anymore.'

'I think I know what you mean. I left London thinking that after a break, I'd go back and start over, doing the same as before but for a different company.' She took a sip of velvety chocolate. 'I'm not sure what that looks like now. It's as if the plan's changed without me deciding to change it. Just from being here.'

'There is something about Iceland. I hesitate to say it but… it's magical…'

They said the words at the same time and sat looking at

each other with their hands around their mugs until Ned took Anna's from her and placed them both back on the table.

He shifted so that he was facing her, with his leg lightly touching the front of her knees.

'Anna, it sounds like a cliche… it is a cliche, but I've never felt like this before.'

Her breath caught in her throat, and she gave a small cough, then giggled, the nerves getting to her. It was suddenly so intense. She didn't want to ruin it.

'I feel like that too, Ned. I have right from when we met at the wedding, but I didn't know what it was then.'

Ned leaned towards her and gently kissed her. It was as if it were the first time again and Anna knew she'd never take that feeling for granted, however many times it might happen in her future.

She kissed him back, putting her hand to the nape of his neck and gently stroking the slight hollow with her thumb.

Ned broke away, pulled the blanket off him, then picked Anna up and laid her on the huge sheepskin rug that was laid in front of the fire.

He kneeled above her, his expression asking for her consent, then when she nodded and smiled, he began to undress her. Once she was naked, she lay there, surprising herself by not feeling at all inhibited, watched him unbutton his fly and then he pulled all of his top layers off in one go, his eyes not moving from hers. His intentions were clear in his gaze; commanding and tender all at once.

'Anna,' he whispered, leaning down over her, his face inches from hers but not quite close enough for her to kiss. 'You might be the woman of my dreams.'

She closed her eyes as he ran his hands down her body until they reached her hips and he lifted her up to meet him.

16

Ned lay on his side, watching Anna sleep. She was beautiful and he couldn't quite believe that she was here. In his bed. The first woman he'd spent the whole night with for a long time. It took him a long time to trust people because you could never tell whether they liked him or the person they thought he was. Anna was the first woman he'd met who he could say with certainty liked him for him and it meant more to him than he'd thought it would. He'd almost resigned himself to never finding that person.

But what this would look like in a couple of months when they both had to get back to the real world, well, that was something that was already starting to worry him. He knew it was crazy to be thinking about that when he'd barely even told Anna that he saw this as something longer term than just a holiday romance that would be over when one of them went home.

It was Saturday but his body clock wasn't taking any notice of that, and he'd woken up as if he were going to the bakery to write. He wanted to and given how deeply Anna was sleeping, he might even make it there and back before she woke up. But instead, he got up, pulled on some joggers and a sweater and made himself a coffee. Then he sat in bed next to her writing until she woke a couple of hours later.

'Morning,' she said, her hand reaching out to touch his leg, her eyes still closed.

He put his notebook down next to the bed and snuggled back down beside her.

'Morning.' He swept her hair away from her forehead and planted a kiss on it. She smiled and opened her eyes.

'You're already up,' she said, taking in his clothes and the fact that he had his glasses on.

'Mm-hmm. I've just been writing some lyrics about a beautiful woman.'

'Oh.' She gave a shy smile and looked away, embarrassed.

'Did I say it was you?' he teased.

She gasped and laughed at him. 'I just assumed.'

'I admit it, you do seem to have become my muse.'

'Any chance the muse could get a cup of coffee?'

Ned rolled his eyes and groaned, enjoying the teasing. He headed into the kitchen, wondering what it would be like to have her around more of the time. He'd tried to keep her at arm's length, partly to play it cool and partly just to see how things went. But after their lunch date, he'd had the hardest time thinking about anything except seeing her again and knew it would be the same the minute she left today. It was great for the writing, but all his new songs were going to be about her at this rate. He was running the risk of turning into a male version of Adele.

He laughed softly to himself and shook his head as he headed back into the bedroom to find Anna flipping through his notebook. He stopped, his first instinct was to be angry and the look on her face told him that she'd seen that emotion briefly in his.

'I'm sorry, Ned. I should have asked you.'

'No, it's okay. I… no one's ever seen my stuff before, that's all. It's not because I don't want you to see it, I've just always kept it to myself.'

She took the coffee off him, unable to meet his eye.

'It's okay, really.' He took her other hand and stroked his thumb across the top, hoping that the gesture would convince her that he didn't mind.

'You write beautiful words, Ned,' she said quietly.

'Thank you. Most of them are about you.'

'Really? I thought you were joking.'

He shook his head. 'Not at all. You've done something to me, Anna. Something that I didn't think anyone would be able to do and something I didn't think I even wanted.'

She looked at him, sincerely. The teasing had stopped, and he was going to tell her. He had to tell her because if she didn't feel the same way, he couldn't risk going any further. It was probably already too far to be unscathed if they weren't on the same page.

'I've avoided relationships, I mean, I've *had* relationships but not this kind. Nothing that meant anything before. I didn't think I would find anyone who could see me, instead of Ned Nokes. And I think you do see me, Anna.'

'It's weird,' she began, 'but although I fancied the pants off the guy that I met at that wedding, it doesn't feel like he's you. You're not Ned Nokes from The Rush, you're just Ned.' She looked straight at him. 'My Ned.'

He kissed her. 'My Anna.'

They spent the rest of the day in bed, alternately making love or he was strumming his guitar and singing tiny bits of songs to her while she suggested additions by way of humming or singing lines with the odd change of words. It was blissful. He never imagined that this could be his life. And it couldn't have been before.

'What will happen when we get back to London?' he asked her later that afternoon.

'I don't know. I don't have a plan for myself, let alone for

what things between us might look like.'
  'But do you see us together?'
  'Yes.'
  That was all he needed to know.

17

Anna had promised Ned that if she tagged along with him to the bakery, she would leave once she'd eaten her breakfast so that he could get on with some writing. As much as she hated getting up early, somehow the prospect of a six o'clock wake-up call was more appealing when it was Ned waking her up.

They sat at his usual table, having both ordered coffee and a cinnamon bun. Ned had wolfed his bun down quickly and his fingers had moved to sit on top of his notebook, poised to begin.

He was watching Anna eat with a lazy smile, indulging her in the fact that she was taking longer than him.

'Sorry, am I holding you up?' she asked, tearing the tiniest piece of dough from her bun and putting it in her mouth.

'No, I could watch you eat all day. In fact, I might write a song about that.'

'Don't waste your time,' she said, knowing that he was teasing. 'No one likes songs about mundane things like eating.'

She could see his brain begin to whirr as he thought of a song which was exactly that, to prove her wrong. He flipped open his notebook and then realising what he'd done, closed it again with a sigh.

'Wow, you really are desperate to get on.'

He shrugged. 'It's a habit now. If I'm in here, I have to write. Nothing I can do about it.'

Anna finished her bun and the last of her coffee.

'It's fine, I'm going now so you can carry on your routine uninterrupted.' She smiled because she loved that he had wanted to have breakfast with her even though it disrupted his usual plan.

He grabbed her hand as she stood up and pulled her to him for a kiss.

'Will you be at home today?'

'Only until lunchtime, then I'm going round to Rachel's to do some wedding stuff. Shall I come round to yours before we go to the open mic night?'

'Yes, that'd be great. I'll cook something.'

'Really?' She couldn't help sounding surprised given that she'd never seen him cook anything before.

'I need the distraction before a gig.'

It seemed odd that Ned seemed to be taking this open mic night thing as seriously as he would any other gig but then it was the first time he'd played in public by himself, with his own material. He was bound to be nervous.

'Okay. I was going to ask Rachel and Jonas if that's alright?'

'Anyone we can rely on to clap rather than boo is very welcome.'

Anna and Ned had just finished eating a simple but delicious pasta dish that he'd cooked for them when the doorbell went.

'Oh, I told Rachel and Jonas to call for us.'

Ned got up, wiping his mouth on a paper napkin as he headed for the intercom. 'Come on up!' he said, buzzing them in.

'I'm starting to think I should have gone by myself, do it

anonymously,' he said as he came back to the kitchen.

'No, it's definitely better to get feedback. If you went on your own, you wouldn't know what people really thought. We'll let you know the word on the street.'

Ned sidled up to Anna, she was still sitting at the breakfast bar. 'I already know you like it, that's enough.'

He looped his hands around her waist, and she placed her hands on his cheeks, pulling him towards her for a kiss.

'Ned, it's going to be great. Everyone will love you and the songs. Have you decided which ones to play?'

He sighed, stepped back and ran his hands through his hair before he started tidying the dishes away. 'No, I think the best song is our song. I'm not sure I can share that one.' He stopped what he was doing and looked at her. 'Can I?'

'Ned,' Anna said softly, 'It's our song, it'll always be our song but it's your song. If you want to share it, you should. You need to play your best stuff, and if that song's your best you'll play it with your heart. Everyone will see that, and they'll love it too.'

He looked at her with a look Anna hadn't seen before but she thought it might be because he loved her. She smiled, blew him a kiss and went to let Rachel and Jonas into the apartment.

'Shall we have a quick drink here before we go?' she asked them all.

'Not for me,' said Ned. 'I think I'll just take a minute to have a practice while you do though.' He disappeared into the bedroom.

'He is nervous?' said Jonas, taking the beer that Anna handed him.

'I think so. It's because it's his new material, it's quite different to The Rush's stuff. I think he worries about what people will make of it.'

'I'm not sure anyone will realise it's him, Anna,' said

Rachel. 'Unless he cuts his hair and takes his glasses off, I think he'll be okay.'

'The people who go to this kind of thing are very supportive,' said Jonas.

'I think that's what made him decide to give it a go. He saw that when we went last week.'

'And we'll be there to support him too,' said Rachel. 'Presumably, you've heard the songs he's going to play?'

'I'm not sure he's decided on what to play yet, but I've heard a few. I think he's amazing.'

'Well, you would,' laughed Rachel. 'We'll give you our unbiased opinion later,' she said, while Jonas shook his head and smiled.

About twenty minutes later Ned emerged from the bedroom and announced that it was time to go. He already had his coat on and his guitar in its case. Anna could see that he was super nervous, all of the colour had drained from his face and his black beanie hat made him look even paler.

'Are you sure?' Anna whispered to him as she pulled her coat on.

He nodded. 'Here is as good a place as any. Better than a roomful of people with expectations of what Ned Nokes is going to do next.'

'Okay. Let's do it then.'

At the bar, Jonas bought drinks for them all while Rachel went to get a table and Ned went to put his name down.

'It's Eddie,' he said when the man with the list asked his name.

Anna smiled at him.

'You are third, Eddie,' said the man.

'Great, thank you.'

They went over to the table that Rachel had found, not right at the front but at the side, a couple of rows back. They'd have a good view of Ned, but he wouldn't see them unless he looked.

'Great table, Rachel,' he said as they sat down.

'Thanks,' she said blushing. 'I thought it would be best if we weren't in your eye line.'

'Third is a good spot, is it?' Anna asked him. He'd visibly relaxed and had even taken a sip of the beer that Jonas had brought him.

'Yeah, I didn't want to be first, but people are still interested enough to listen at that point in the evening.'

She pulled off his beanie hat and ruffled his hair to make it less flat. 'Well, you look fab. You'll be brilliant.'

But once the second act was on, he began to get fidgety and was fiddling with the strap on his guitar until Anna took his hand and squeezed it.

Everyone applauded the man and woman duo who had just finished, then the compere shouted, 'Eddie! You are up!'

Ned gave her a quick kiss on the cheek and made his way to the small stage at the front, next to the bar. He sat on a stool, with his guitar resting on his knee, and pulled the microphone nearer to him

'Hi, I'm Eddie from London. I'm here on holiday for a few weeks and have been finding Iceland great for my creative juices.'

A low ripple of laughter went through the audience along with a few appreciative claps.

'This one's called The Light Inside.'

The song was one Anna had heard bits of before, but not the whole thing. It was the first time she'd seen him perform in front of anyone but her and she was overwhelmed by his presence. No one seemed to know who he was but there was something there, a level of certainty, showmanship even, that was unmistakable. If anything was likely to give him away, it was that.

Rachel caught her eye and gave an enthusiastic nod, her

eyes wide. Anna felt enormous pride that this was her boyfriend, and he was going to take the world by storm with his amazing talent. One day soon, everyone in this room would remember that they'd seen Ned playing his new stuff in a tiny bar in Reykjavik where no one knew who he was.

The applause after the first song was incredible considering that there couldn't have been more than a hundred people in the room. Ned sat there grinning and nodding graciously to everyone. Then he caught Anna's eye and she knew he was okay. He was happy with how it was going.

Once the applause had died down, Ned waited a few seconds before he started playing his next song.

'This is called Waves from the Storm,' he said into the microphone, over the melody he was playing. Anna's chest contracted. It was their song. He was doing it.

The song was as perfect as Anna remembered. Almost more so because Ned was sharing it. It was as if he was telling the whole room that he loved her. That she was his.

It was over all too soon and the crowd were stamping, clapping and whistling. It seemed to go on and on. Ned had stood up and bowed and now was grinning like a Cheshire Cat as he made his way back to their table with people clapping him on the back all the way.

He sat down and took a long drink from his beer.

'Eddie, everyone!' said the compere. 'One to look out for!'

'Oh my god, Ned, they love you,' Rachel said, looking almost as happy as he did.

'Yeah, I think it went well,' he said modestly, even though his face said that he knew he'd killed it.

He turned to Anna and gave her a very intense kiss, considering they were out in public. But he was on a high. This was a turning point for him, giving him the validation he needed to know he was on the right track, and that what he wanted to write was what people wanted to hear. It was clear from his face that this was what he lived for, and she may not have been the biggest fan of The Rush to be able to know for sure, but she was pretty certain that he'd never had a moment quite as amazing as this before.

They stayed to enjoy the rest of the evening, chatting during the breaks with Jonas and Rachel like any group of friends, not ones who didn't know each other all that well. Anna didn't think she'd ever had a night out like this before. She'd never been with anyone long enough to get to the point of wanting to hang out with another couple, and besides, Rachel was going out with Adam who shared a mutual dislike of her so double dates had never been an option before.

'Eddie!' called the guy who'd been compering and was in charge of the list of acts. 'See you next week?'

Ned gave him a thumbs up and a kind of salute-slash-wave that pop stars do when they go off stage. 'Sure thing, man.'

Anna laughed.

'What?' he said, laughing too.

'You're not going to be incognito for very long, Ned.'

'Watch me,' he said, giving her a playful shove as they made their way back towards his place.

They got to the corner where Rachel and Jonas would head back to theirs.

'Thanks, Ned. It was a great night,' said Jonas, hugging Ned and slapping him on the back.

'Ah, thanks for coming, guys. If you're up for it next week, that'd be amazing. Maybe ask Brun and the others?'

'Leave it with me. I will spread the word,' said Jonas.

18

Ned spent the next few days on a high from playing at the bar.

'I played an open mic night,' he blurted out as soon as Freddie picked up his FaceTime call the following day.

'By yourself? What did you play?'

'The guitar, obviously.'

'No, you div. I mean, what tracks?'

'I'm calling them numbers these days.'

Freddie laughed. 'Whatever, Neddy boy. New stuff or were you playing it safe with covers?'

'New stuff. I wrote it here. It's a bit different to what I was writing before. I've definitely taken a turn towards the folk.'

'Blimey. And how did it go? I'm imagining not too bad, otherwise you'd be keeping it quiet.'

'Yeah, amazing, Fred. I'm still on a high now. I've never known anything like it, not even playing the biggest stadiums in the world gave me a buzz like I had last night.'

'Oh, playing at the O2 isn't amazing anymore?'

'Come on, you know it is. I just mean it's different. Playing your own stuff, it makes a difference when people love it. They love the music, they don't care who's playing it.'

'They don't know it's you? Because I could totally believe

that's the case. You're starting to look like a bespectacled yeti.'

'It's cold here, facial hair gains new importance in Iceland. But yeah, no one knows it's me, apart from Anna and her friends. I called myself Eddie.'

'That's almost our couple name. I'm touched. And you and Anna are going out properly now? When did that happen?'

'I don't know, I guess I asked her on a date, and it just went on from there.'

'Good for you. And she was there for the debut of your new stuff. That says a lot.'

Ned shrugged and smiled. 'Yeah, it does.'

'Does it?' Freddie's eyes were wide. 'It's like, serious?'

'Could be.'

The open mic night had gone better than he could have imagined, and he was working on two new songs for the next one. If he could get a couple of new ones ready each week, he'd have a really good idea of which songs resonated the most with people by the time he went back to London. And Anna being there, sharing that with him, was pretty unbelievable. He felt as if she understood him, had his back and was the support he needed to give him the confidence to put himself out there.

Anna had been amazing. She'd gone along with whatever he wanted over the past week or so. Leaving him alone when he wanted to write, only staying over when he suggested it, never really making any calls on him at all. Which was kind of odd, especially compared to most of the women he'd tangled with in the past. Was he being selfish? Taking exactly what he wanted from her without considering what her needs might be? He was suddenly filled with a need to tell her, show her that he wasn't that guy. He needed her to know that he appreciated her more than he could say. That she was the reason he was on cloud nine right now.

He called Brun.

'Hey, how's it going?'

'Ned, I heard good things about your gig.'

'Thanks, I hope you'll come along next week?'

'Sure thing. So, what can I do for you?'

'I'm thinking of going on a Northern Lights excursion.'

Once he'd made the arrangements with Brun, he texted Anna and told her he'd be picking her up for dinner and to wear all of her clothes because it would be cold. He could picture her laughing as she read it.

As soon as he saw the vehicle that Brun had organised, Ned knew he was onto a winner. It was a Jeep on steroids.

'Hello, I'm Siggi,' said the driver, holding the back door open for Ned.

'Ned. Thanks, man.' He shook Siggi's hand and climbed into the comfortable back seat. There was a bottle of champagne and two glasses in a caddy on the floor and there was shadow lighting around the carpeted area in front of the seat so that it wasn't completely dark.

They drove towards Rachel's house, having to go around in a circle because of the one-way system of tiny streets around her house.

'I won't be a sec,' said Ned, heading up the cobbled path to collect her. He walked towards the fairy-lit garden and could see Anna looking out for him. She waved and then the lights inside the house went off before she opened the door.

Ned could barely tell it was her, she was so wrapped up in a hat, what could easily have been more than one scarf and her usual enormous coat.

'Ready?' he asked.

'Definitely.' She locked the door and then pulled him in for a kiss. 'Do you think you have enough clothes on?' She frowned as she looked at him.

'I've left some of my stuff in the car, it's cosy in there.'

'Let's go then.'

Ned took her hand and led her to the Jeep where Siggi was waiting to open the door.

'Oh my goodness, this is cool!'

'Cool is exactly what I was going for.'

They got into the back and once they were on their way, he opened the champagne.

'Here's to us,' he said, loving that Anna's eyes mirrored exactly how he was feeling.

'To us.'

'*Skál!*' Siggi called from the front.

They both laughed and repeated it. 'How could we have forgotten?' said Ned.

'So where are we off to?' Anna asked.

'It's a surprise,' said Ned. 'I hope it'll be a night to remember for both of us.'

The drive was around half an hour. When Siggi pulled up in a deserted car park, there was a faint glow of light coming from behind a row of trees.   'This is really exciting,' said Anna, which was a relief because Ned was more nervous than excited. He'd never done a grand gesture for anyone if that's even what this was. It felt like a lot was riding on it, which was weird because he knew Anna wasn't with him for the money or the lifestyle. He just wanted her to have an amazing night.

'Okay guys,' said Siggi. 'I'll see you in a couple of hours.'

They pulled on their hats and scarves and shoved their gloves in their pockets just in case. Anna's eyes were shining as she took his hand and they headed along the path towards a glass building that was glowing in the darkness.

'It looks like a greenhouse,' Anna said, looking questioningly at Ned.

'It is a greenhouse. Brun recommended it.'

She frowned, understandably not quite clear on why what

made a greenhouse a destination for their night out. Once Ned had opened the door, it all became clear. It was literally a greenhouse, with the unmistakable smell of tomatoes filling the air, taking him back to his childhood when he used to help his grandad water his tomatoes. That was enough to make it a great place for an outing. But there was more to it than that. Nestled on a pathway between the vines that reached right to the roof, was a table for two. There were other tables at one end of the greenhouse, so it was obviously a restaurant during the day but tonight they had it to themselves.

A waiter greeted them as they made their way across and sat down. There were tiny fairy lights twisted amongst the vines next to them, and the look on Anna's face made him glad that he'd trusted Brun to choose the perfect venue. It was also lovely and warm.

'Ned, this is fabulous. A once-in-a-lifetime kind of thing.'

'I want it to be a special night. You've been amazing, Anna. I know we haven't been together that long but the support you give me… and you never expect anything.'

She shrugged. 'I just love being with you Ned, so I'm happy with however that looks.'

Ned was about to explain to her that their relationship needn't be on his terms when their waiter, who introduced himself as Magnus, produced a bottle of wine.

'Wine?' he asked, poised to pour it into the glasses that were already on the table.

'Yes, please.'

'Are you ready for the first course?'

While they waited for whatever the food was because there was no menu, Ned attempted to tell Anna what he wanted to say.

'I think I'm used to people revolving around me, do you know what I mean?'

She nodded. 'That's probably normal when you're a pop star.'

'But I don't want you to do that. I… we need to be in it together. You deserve whatever you want from me. I've been dictating the course of things and that's going to change.'

Magnus delivered bowls of steaming tomato soup to them, explaining that it was accompanied by bread that had been cooked in the ground from the natural geothermal heat.

He tried again, in between bites of the delicious bread. 'That open mic night was a game changer for me. I'd been obsessing about the music, about what was next.'

'And it paid off.'

He grinned, surprised that he could understand her given the amount of food in her mouth.

'You can take your time. Don't worry, I'll deck Magnus if he tries to whip it away. Thanks, it did pay off and things feel different now. That's all going to be okay, I know that now. And now there's you.'

Anna gave a lop-sided, slightly bashful smile. 'That sounds nice, Ned. So that's what tonight is about?'

'Yes. Tonight is me showing you that I appreciate everything you've done for me.'

She reached for his hand across the table and squeezed it. 'Thanks, Ned. You didn't need to. I came to Iceland in a bit of a mess now that I look back on it. You're the first man I've ever been remotely serious about, and I have no expectations about what a relationship looks like. It's working for us and I'm happy, I think we're both happy.'

She gave him a questioning look and he nodded.

'So that's the only thing that matters.'

Magnus cleared their empty bowls and announced that the next course was ready.

'You're serious about me?'

He was fishing. He wanted to know what she thought of

their relationship, lay it all out so they both knew where they stood. But he knew now she'd said that, that he was on safe ground.

'Yes, I am,' she said, taking a sip of wine. 'And now I know you feel the same.' She rolled her eyes around the scene before them and looked pointedly at him.

'Got nothing to hide,' he said, reaching for her hand.

'And you don't think it's too quick or that it's just because we're both here with not much else going on?'

'Does it matter if it is that? We've had time to get to know each other. It could have taken months to get to this point if we'd met in our normal lives. I know for me, that's one reason why I've never had a proper relationship with anyone before.'

'Unwilling to put the time in?' she teased, her eyes wandering to the dished Magnus was now delivering to them.

He laughed, 'I didn't have time, that was the problem.'

'So, you're telling me you've been celibate the whole time you were in the band?'

'I think you know that's unlikely. That's one of the biggest perks of being in a band.'

Anna laughed. 'That's what I thought.'

The main course was a delicious cheese-filled ravioli with a rich tomato sauce and was full of flavour.

'I'm joking. I mean, I could have had my pick of girls. That makes me sound like a dick, but you know what I mean.'

'I do. And I know you're not a dick, Ned. So that's why you didn't find anyone. Because that's not how you find… this.'

Once they'd eaten their dessert of a surprisingly tasty tomato ice cream, they bid Magnus good night and headed outside in search of Siggi.

'That was so cool, Ned. Thanks.'

Ned put his arm around her shoulders and pulled her into him. She rested her head on his shoulder, the wool of her hat tickling his cheek, making him smile. And Ned thought that he'd never be happier than he was right at this moment.

Just five minutes after they left the greenhouse, Siggi pulled over.

'Okay, guys, we are going Northern Lights hunting.'

'Really?' Anna said enthusiastically, pulling her coat, gloves, hat and scarf back on before Siggi had even turned the engine off.

They walked through the darkness until they could both see some faint lights a little way off. Once they got closer, Ned could see a circle of lanterns with a big pile of blankets stacked in the centre. They got themselves settled, with blankets wrapped around their shoulders and other blankets that they sat on top of, and then Siggi produced a couple of flasks and poured a cup of steaming hot berry juice for each of them. He then turned out the lanterns so that there was no light pollution, sat back down and said, 'now we wait.'

It didn't take very long before he pointed out a glimpse of green, almost like a small green cloud in the dark of the sky. Then they watched as it expanded into curtain-like waves of green and purple, rippling in front of their eyes.

'It's unbelievable,' Anna said quietly. 'More amazing than I imagined it would be.'

Ned noticed Siggi slink away from them.

'I'm glad we've seen them together for the first time, it makes it more special.'

He wrapped his arm around her and gently pulled her to the ground so that they were lying, cosy in their blanket nest, watching the most spectacular show on earth. Together.

19

Rachel, Gudrun and Anna were round at Rachel's house doing some wedding planning. The important stuff like the venue, the food and the band had already been sorted out by Rachel and Jonas as soon as he'd proposed but the little details were still being finalised and Rachel had insisted that they needed a wedding committee meeting.

'So, Gudrun, are you okay with getting the candles for the table centrepieces from Snug? And we can go to the restaurant the day before and set it all up.'

The reception was being held at a restaurant which as far as Anna could gather, was in the middle of nowhere but was something to do with the night that Rachel and Jonas got stuck in a snowstorm, around the time they got together.

'Yes, I will put them on order tomorrow. That is fine. But also, I need to hear from Anna about the special trip that Ned had Brun organise.'

Rachel sighed. 'Five-minute break but then we have to talk about the hen night.'

'Deal. So, Anna, what was it? Olafur did not know exactly. Was it a Northern Lights excursion?'

Anna explained the evening to Gudrun and Rachel.

'And afterwards, we did see the Northern Lights. Siggi

said it was very early in the season for such a spectacular display.'

'That is fate, Anna,' said Gudrun, all wide-eyed and dreamy. 'It is the spirits telling you that your relationship with Ned is blessed. That is just what happened to Rachel and Jonas.'

'It's not quite the same,' Rachel said, flipping through her notepad. Gudrun rolled her eyes, 'It is,' she insisted. 'Anna had her magical moment with Ned. It is just the same as yours with Jonas.'

'Well, it is hard to hold onto the magic when you've just moved house and are getting married. It's stressful.'

Anna felt guilty that she'd not been more helpful to Rachel. The wedding seemed to have been ticking along in the background but with moving as well, it was bound to feel overwhelming.

'Sorry, Rach. You're so good at being organised, I forget that maybe it's not as effortless as you make it look.'

Rachel smiled. 'I'm sorry. It just feels like everything's coming at me a bit too quickly. Jonas has organised so much of the wedding but that just makes me feel a bit out of control.'

'Let us make the important plans,' said Gudrun. 'The hen night. I am thinking we should go to the Sky Lagoon,' said Gudrun. 'I know you would like something to do with water and the Secret Lagoon is too far to ask everyone to go.'

'Do you think so? I would love the Secret Lagoon. Also, do you think it's mad to have a joint hen and stag night? It kind of seems like a shame not to celebrate with everyone.'

'Unconventional, but it's a great idea,' said Anna. 'They're all your friends, why be sexist for the sake of tradition? Do you think Jonas will be up for that?'

'Why don't we have a party all together somewhere like the gin bar?' Gudrun suggested.

Anything that didn't involve her having to get wet seemed like a good idea, so Anna backed the gin bar idea.

'Basically, we need somewhere to drink and chat, maybe have a dance later on,' she said.

'You're right, let's go with the gin bar and I'll see what Jonas thinks. Have you heard whether they have anything organised yet, Gudrun?'

Gudrun shook her head. 'They are men, Rachel. They have not even thought about it yet. I will go and see Gunnar and make a booking. He might let us have the mezzanine to ourselves,' said Gudrun, making a note on her phone.

'And what about the dress, Rach? You must have that organised by now, but you haven't mentioned it. That's got to be right up there with one of the most important things to sort out.'

Rachel grimaced. 'You're going to think I've lost my mind when I tell you this, but you have to trust me.' She glared at Anna and Gudrun, daring them to challenge her.

'I love your clothes, Rachel,' said Gudrun. 'I can just imagine you have chosen a 1960s vintage dress.'

'Not quite, Gudrun but I appreciate your faith.'

Anna laughed. 'I have the faith!'

'You hate all my clothes!' Rachel said, laughing but trying to be cross. 'That's why I haven't told you because you'll think I'm a nutter!'

'Try me. It can't be any worse than you wearing those comfy shoes,' Anna made air quotes with her fingers, 'to every club we've ever been to together.'

'She hates my brogues,' Rachel explained to Gudrun.

'You cannot wear shoes like that to a club in London?' Gudrun looked confused.

'Not unless you want everyone to think you're in fancy dress.'

'That is so harsh! They're comfortable and practical and I

don't see you wearing high heels these days, Anna.'

'The chance would be a fine thing. Does anyone here wear heels?'

'Not very often,' Gudrun said, with a look of sad resignation.

'But we will for the wedding, right Gudrun? I mean, you must be, Rach, on your wedding day of all days.'

'Nope. Definitely don't want to break an ankle on my wedding day of all days.'

'And what about the dress?' Gudrun said, bringing the conversation back on topic.

'It's knitted. And before you say anything, it's beautiful. It's not like anything you can imagine.'

Anna didn't know what to say. Rachel had always had a more eclectic taste in clothes than she did but a knitted wedding dress. Had she been brainwashed by an Icelandic knitter?

'Well, that's...'

'It's a wonderful idea!' said Gudrun enthusiastically.

'I saw this woman on Instagram who had knitted her own wedding dress and it was just the most perfect dress I'd ever seen. And wool makes sense as we're getting married in November.'

'You're not knitting it yourself,' Anna said in disbelief. She was impressed with Rachel's relatively newly acquired knitting skills but there was a big difference between a hat, or even a jumper, and a whole dress.

'No,' Rachel laughed. 'Katrin at the wool shop put me in touch with someone who is making it. It's almost finished. But the best thing is that I've been able to choose quite a few of the details. The sleeves are in a traditional Icelandic lace pattern that I've chosen, it's so pretty.'

'It sounds beautiful, Rachel. I cannot wait to see it,' said Gudrun.

* * *

'How's the wedding prep going?' Ned asked when they were eating dinner at Anna's later that evening.

'Yes, okay. The wedding dress is… very Icelandic.'

'Sounds interesting. What about the most important part, the hen night?'

Anna dished another spoonful of pasta bake onto each of their plates.

'We're going to the gin bar, wherever that is, and I think Rachel's going to suggest a joint hen and stag do.'

'That's a bit different.'

'I think the bar sounds a bit like any other night out, but I don't know what else to suggest. I mean, I could organise a fantastic hen night in London, no problem, but here is different. Gudrun wondered about going to the Secret Lagoon which sounds quite exciting, but then she decided it was too far.'

Ned put his fork down and took a sip of wine, looking thoughtful.

'Do you think it would be… overstepping if I sorted something for everyone?'

'You want to organise the hen and stag nights?' Anna looked at him in amusement. 'And what qualifications do you have to take that on?'

'I did a pretty good job of organising Freddie's. We had a brilliant time,' he said grinning and shaking his head as he took another sip of wine. 'Let me pitch the idea to Brun and see what he thinks. If it's a goer, I'll let you in on the plan.'

'Okay, let me know and then I'll talk to Gudrun before she books the gin bar.'

'That's settled then.'

'Did you have a productive day?'

Ned nodded enthusiastically with a mouthful of food.

'I think I have a great song worked out ready for the next

open mic night.'

'Is it about me?' It might be the best feeling in the world to have a boyfriend who wrote songs for you, about you.

'They can't all be about you, lovely.'

'Well, I look forward to hearing it anyway,' she smiled. 'Do you want to stay tonight? It's closer to the bakery.'

It was the first time she'd suggested that Ned stay at her place. It was more homely than his, but she didn't know what he thought about it. The bed was smaller, and everything was a bit more lived in.

'That'd be great, thanks.' He got up from the table, leaned over and kissed her, then picked up the plates and took them over to the sink.

'You don't have to do that,' Anna said, leaping up.

'No, you cooked, I'll clean,' he said. But he did put the plates down to take her in his arms. 'How domesticated are we?'

'I think we make a good team,' Anna replied, looking into his eyes and seeing that maybe he didn't want to clean up right now.

'We do.' He kissed her. 'Hang on.' He pulled away and took his phone out of his pocket. 'It's Freddie. I should take this.'

He took his phone into the lounge and Anna began tidying the kitchen, trying not to listen to his call but easily able to hear his side of the conversation.

'I spoke to her, Fred. I thought everything was okay.'

Now she was listening. Who was he talking about?

'Has anyone sussed out that I'm here? I don't want her to find out, she was on about coming over.'

Anna tried to remember what Ned had said about his previous girlfriends. She was sure he hadn't mentioned anyone in particular, he'd just alluded to the fact that there hadn't been anyone serious. Now she was wondering if that was true. After all, why would the woman he was talking to Freddie about want to come and visit him if there was nothing between them?

'Let me know if you hear anything. Thanks, man.'

'Is everything alright?' Anna asked when Ned came back into the kitchen.

'Yes, Freddie was just giving me a heads up about something.'

Oh. So that was it. She'd gathered more from the accidental eavesdropping than she had from what Ned was willing to tell her.

'Right.'

Anna began washing up and Ned picked up a cloth to begin drying. He was distracted, fiddling with the corner of the tea towel, deep in thought.

'I might take a rain check on tonight and head home.'

He put the tea towel down and was already pulling his coat on.

'Okay. Maybe see you tomorrow.'

'I'll call you.'

'We're still going to the open mic night?'

'Of course.' He pulled his hat on and came over to kiss her.

'Ned, is everything okay? I heard— '

'Everything's fine, Anna. I'll see you tomorrow.'

She watched from the window as he walked down the path. His hands in his pockets and his head down. She could tell from his stance that he was feeling defeated, not the upbeat Ned she had grown to love over the past few weeks. And she was sad that he wouldn't share that with her. It surprised and hurt that he'd shut her out when it seemed like he needed someone to talk to.

She sat on the sofa, pulled a blanket around her shoulders, and picked up her phone.

I hope you're okay, I'm here if you need to talk x

He wouldn't be home yet and maybe wouldn't see her message until he was. She pulled out her laptop and started watching an episode of Gilmore Girls, her go-to comfort viewing.

Two episodes later, she still hadn't had a response from Ned. Whatever he'd found out on that call had shaken him. Enough to pull away from her.

20

The next day, Anna woke up early enough to know that she'd catch Ned if she went to the bakery. She hadn't slept well, mulling over the phone call that had had such an effect on him. More than anything, she wanted to just come out and ask him what it was about but as she'd tried that once and he'd brushed it off, she didn't feel able to do it again. Another brush-off would feel a lot worse.

But she needed to see him, to make sure he was okay. If there was something he was struggling with, she wanted to be there for him. Maybe he wasn't used to having someone he could lean on. She might need to spell it out for him.

Anna pulled on her warmest clothes. Now that it was October, it was still dark at six in the morning and the days were a lot colder in general. She pulled the front door closed behind her and headed towards the bakery. For the first time since she'd arrived in Iceland, she noticed her breath making clouds when she exhaled. That hardly ever happened in London, or not that she noticed at least.

The smell of the bakery drifted along the road and Anna was ravenous by the time she walked in. The woman behind the counter recognised her with a smile. Before placing her order, Anna glanced over to the seating area, but Ned wasn't there.

'Not today,' said the woman with a rueful smile.

Anna managed a smile and ordered two cinnamon buns to take away. She'd fully expected Ned to be there. It was his routine, and he hadn't strayed from it until now. Even when she'd stayed over at his, he'd still come here to write every morning and the fact that he hadn't this morning could only be a bad sign.

She needed to talk to someone, so she headed to Rachel's. It was too early, and she had to wait a few minutes periodically knocking on the door and texting, but Rachel eventually answered.

'You'd better have a good reason, Anna.' She left the door open for Anna to follow her inside, but she looked barely awake.

'Go and sit in the lounge and I'll make the coffee. I bought you a cinnamon bun. Has Jonas gone to work?' Because she only had two buns.

'Mmm.' Rachel looked as if she was going to go back to sleep in the corner of the sofa.

Anna made the coffee and put the buns on tea plates.

'Ned had a call yesterday from Freddie.'

That woke Rachel up. 'Freddie from The Rush?'

'Yes. I heard what Ned was saying to him. It was something about a woman. He was asking Freddie if she knew where he was because she wanted to come and visit him.'

'Right. So, you're wondering who the woman is. Did you ask him?'

'He went into the lounge to take the call, so I think he assumes I didn't hear but I asked if everything was okay, and he said yes but then he left even though he was going to stay the night.'

'Have you done the most obvious thing and googled him?'

Anna was annoyed at not having thought of that herself. 'No.'

Rachel reached for her laptop.

'Are you sure it's a good idea?' said Anna. 'What if he has a girlfriend and didn't tell me?'

'Then you'll know that he has a girlfriend and didn't tell you. If you're dating a celebrity, this is a fast-track way to find out what's going on. There's no need to rely on your friend being in the right place at the right time to find these things out.'

'Okay.' She'd much rather find out from google if Ned had a girlfriend than go through the humiliation of being oblivious. That had happened to Rachel with her last boyfriend and Anna had been the one to tell her.

'The good news is that the consensus of the media is that he's single,' Rachel announced after a couple of minutes.

'What's the bad news?'

'There are a lot of photos of him with a woman called Jeannie Fenton, she's on the PR team of The Rush by the looks of things.'

Rachel turned the laptop so that Anna could see. There were several photos of Ned with a petite blond woman. They weren't holding hands or anything else that suggested they were a couple. In fact, in most of the pictures, they were in a larger group with the rest of the band.

'She's pretty,' said Anna, glumly.

'I'm not sure this is conclusive proof that there's anything between them.'

Rachel began rooting around in a basket of magazines and pulled out the copy of Hey! that had Freddie's wedding in.

'If they're together, she'll be at the wedding do, in the background at least. Everyone wants to go with someone to a wedding.'

They scanned the pictures and sure enough in an action

shot of Freddie and Sophia on the dance floor, Anna spotted Ned.

'There he is.' It was the back of someone, a man, with his partner's hands looped around his neck.

'Really? How can you tell?'

'That's him. His suit, the way his hair was on that day. And he's dancing with her.'

'He's dancing with someone,' said Rachel, gently pulling the magazine out of Anna's hands and putting it away.

'He said he'd never had a proper relationship because he finds it difficult to trust women. Do you think she's like a regular booty call?' It sounded so unsavoury. So un-Ned.

'Maybe. In his situation, I'm sure it would be fairly easy to have that kind of arrangement with someone.'

'And she wants to come and see him. I don't think that is a booty call, Rach. That's a woman who's missing him.'

'You need to talk to him.'

Anna groaned and put her head in her hands. The open mic night was tonight, and they were supposed to be going together and with the whole gang this time. Assuming he would even turn up, it would be so awkward if they hadn't spoken at all beforehand.

'He said he'd call me today. I'll wait until he does and then go round and have it out.'

'Okay, that's a good plan. And then ring me and tell me what happened.'

Anna walked back to her house feeling not much better than when she'd left earlier that morning. At least she had more of an idea of what she might be dealing with but no real clue why Ned had got so funny about it. Her main worry was that perhaps he did have a relationship with this woman in London and that she was waiting for him while he was squirrelled away in Iceland, writing. His two worlds were completely separate at the moment so it might have been easy to see Anna as a holiday romance. But he had asked what would happen when they got back to London. Anna had thought that meant that their relationship would continue but maybe he was just weighing up his options.

Or was it that the possibility of this woman wanting to come here to see him was making him feel like his old life was catching up with him again, a bit like the night in the bar when the band had started playing a cover version of one of The Rush's songs. His strict routine and isolating himself here where no one knew him smacked of someone who was almost running away from something.

She busied herself for the rest of the morning responding to enquiries from her marketing campaign to tour companies and now she even had a couple of confirmed dates to forward to Rachel to organise more fully with the clients. Just after lunch, she was still engrossed in setting up some social media channels for Rachel when her phone buzzed with a text from Ned.

Just checking we are still on for tonight. See you there?

On one hand, she was glad that he was still planning to play and had assumed that she was still going. On the other hand, she was annoyed that he didn't want to see, or seemingly talk to her today. There wouldn't be much opportunity tonight and maybe that's what he was hoping for.

Fine for later but will come to yours with dinner x

The night when they'd had dinner at the tomato greenhouse, he'd said that he was aware that he had been dictating the course of their time together and that he'd known that was unfair. Yet here he was trying to control it again. Well, no, sorry Ned. Not everything can be on your terms.

He didn't respond so at five o'clock Anna got herself ready and picked up some fish and chips from Fish and Co. which was on her way.

He opened the door looking sheepish and Anna handed him the bag of food so that she could take her coat and shoes off. She was feeling feisty. It was the first time she'd felt like that since she'd been in Iceland. The first time she'd needed to, normally it was a feeling that only manifested itself when she dealt with difficult people at work, or Rachel's ex-boyfriend, Adam. She hadn't expected Ned to draw out this side of herself, but she felt ready to confront him.

He was arranging the food onto two plates as she walked into the kitchen.

'Good day?' She kept her tone breezy, almost daring him to ignore the definite atmosphere that was between them.

'I've just been practising. Look, Anna. About last night.'

He clearly thought that she would leap in and say something at this point, but she didn't. He didn't seem like he was about to say anything else either but then realising that she was looking at him, waiting for him to continue, he did.

'Um, Fred rang to say that this girl I sometimes… see. She's been asking around about me. I spoke to her a couple of weeks ago and made it clear that there's nothing between us anymore but she's still trying to find out where I am.'

'Right. So, you're not in a relationship with her.'

'No, I never was. But,' he ran his hands through his hair in exasperation, 'it's one of those situations where I guess I thought we were both on the same page and it turns out perhaps she thought it was more than it was.'

Anna couldn't help feeling sorry for him, but she didn't let on. It would have been easy to take him in her arms and have that be the end of the explanation but there was more at stake than Ned upsetting some girl. This was about him handling a situation that potentially affected both of them. Anna hadn't been in PR for ten years without knowing that his every move mattered. Whether he'd left the band or not, the public interest in him would be at an all-time high. The fact that this woman, Jeannie, also worked in PR made Anna think that she might be asking around for Ned's whereabouts so that she could leak it to the press as a form of revenge.

'So, you spoke to her and explained. How did she take that?'

'Not great, to be honest. Stuff like that never goes well, does it?'

'Do you think she might be trying to hurt you by finding out where you are so that she can leak it?'

Ned's eyes widened. 'That makes sense. Freddie said she won't let it go, has been spreading the word that I'm in hiding somewhere and he said that there's started to be more interest in me in the media over the past couple of days.'

He pushed the plates over the breakfast bar to where Anna was perched on a stool, then stood with his head in his hands for a few seconds.

'Shit, Anna. This is going to ruin everything. She's going to take this away from me.'

Anna stood up and took him in her arms. Now she knew where they stood, she could do that. He needed her.

'No. She isn't. What did Freddie say?'

She gently pulled him to sit down on the stool next to her and she began eating, hoping that he would do the same.

'He said he'd spoken to the team, and they'd suggested I put out a statement to say that I'm somewhere else concentrating on writing new material. I don't want to work with them, Anna. I don't trust them, Jeannie's on that team.'

'Okay. So, we put out our own statement. I can do that for you. Forget using your old team. You have a new one now.'

Ned smiled gratefully and picked up his fork. 'Thanks, Anna. It never crossed my mind that you'd be able to help, and I didn't want to dump my problems on you just because we're... together.'

'That's what being together is about, Ned. I know neither of us is used to having someone to lean on like that, but that's what we have now.'

'Are you sure we can do this by ourselves?'

It was then that Anna realised that she'd glossed over what she actually did. Ned probably thought she worked for the photographer or the wedding planner, not a PR company. But she didn't anymore so there was no point mentioning it.

'We definitely can.'

'Thank you. That's amazing, it's such a relief.'

'That's okay. Write me another song as a thank you.'

He laughed and Anna could feel that they were back to where they'd been.

21

If the first open mic night was a confirmation to Ned that he was going in the right direction, the second was a resounding success. Whether it was because he knew what to expect this time or if it was because of the support from his friends and Anna, he didn't know. But the vibe was working for him, and he even got a standing ovation. After the first time, the guy who organised the running order had taken a punt and put him at the end knowing that word may have spread that he was worth waiting for. The risk had paid off and it was the best way to finish the night, sending everyone home on a high.

As they left, a woman approached Ned and asked him for his autograph.

'Oh, sure,' he said, giving her an uncertain smile while everyone in the group, aside from Anna, Rachel and Jonas, were making faces as if it were mad that anyone would want the autograph of a person who had played a couple of open mic nights.

'She thinks you are the next big thing,' said Brun, clapping Ned on the back. They'd decided to head to the gin bar to celebrate Ned's success.

'Some people in the UK know who I am, she's probably on

holiday and recognised me.'

'Ah, I knew you had something about you, Ned. Is that why you go by Eddie in the bar?'

Ned nodded. 'It's easier if people don't know.'

Brun looked at him quizzically. 'How famous are you?'

'Have you heard of The Rush?'

'The boy band? Yes… but…'

'I was in that band. That Ned. But undercover, in Iceland.'

'Fjandinn mér,' Brun said, shaking his head. 'I did not know. Your music is so different to that.'

'That's the idea. Making my own way now instead of following the plan, you know?'

'I do, Ned.' He gave a deep laugh. 'I cannot believe I was fooled by a pair of glasses and a patchy beard!'

'I don't mind if you guys know but I'm trying to keep it quiet that I'm here. So far no one at home knows and it's better for everyone if it stays like that.'

'No problem, Ned. You are safe with us.'

And Ned felt safe. For the first time in a long time. These people were genuine, and he knew that knowing who he really was wouldn't change anything. It meant a lot to him that Rachel and Jonas respected his privacy enough to not even have spoken about him amongst their friends.

The gin bar was relatively quiet. The gang seemed to know the people who worked there and aside from asking Ned and Anna what they would like, it seemed unnecessary for anyone else to say what they wanted.

'This is where the hen night is going to be,' said Anna as they gathered a couple of extra stools to go around the high table that they'd commandeered.

'It's pretty cool,' said Ned. It was a mixture of Nordic decor, with lots of wooden furniture, sheepskins and reindeer hides on the seats but with a modern twist; a huge wall of bottles, all different colours which were lit so that they glowed quite spectacularly.

'Definitely very different to anywhere in London,' said Anna.

'I still haven't spoken to Brun, but I do have a proper plan now.'

Ned explained what his plan was. 'I'll talk to Brun tonight.'

'That sounds amazing, but we can't let you do that.'

'I want to. These people, and especially Jonas and Rachel have made me so welcome. You know they hadn't told anyone who I am? I owe them.'

Anna nodded to show she understood. 'As soon as Brun's on board, I'll tell Jonas and Rachel that we're sorting the hen and stag.'

Ned grinned. He was thrilled to be able to do something to thank them and moved around the table to sit next to Brun to see what he thought.   'That is very generous, Ned. If you had suggested that before I knew who you were, I would have refused. But now…' He laughed.

'I'm glad to do it.' This bunch of people who had welcomed him so warmly were the closest to a group of friends that Ned had ever had outside of the band, and it was something rare. Something he knew he would miss when it was time to leave.

22

Jonas and Rachel loved the idea of a surprise joint hen and stag party. Rachel was so anxious about the wedding day going smoothly, her relatives being able to get here from the UK now that the risk of snow was ever present, that she was just glad to have the chance of a break that someone else had organised.

Brun had organised a minibus for them and all they knew was to bring an overnight bag with clothes to dress for dinner and their swimming stuff.

Anna and Ned had walked to Rachel and Jonas's house so that Siggi as the designated driver and only single person on the trip, had fewer pickups to do.

'While we're waiting, Anna, come and see the dress,' said Rachel.

'Beer, Ned?' Jonas asked, wandering into the kitchen.

Rachel led the way upstairs and into the spare room which was still full of unpacked boxes and had a garment bag hanging on the back of the door.

'Oh my god, Rach, it's absolutely beautiful!'

Rachel had just pulled one of the sleeves out. It was delicate ivory lace knitting with a slight fuzz to the yarn that made it look ethereal.

'That's all you get. I just wanted you to see that it wasn't weird.'

'I retract everything I thought about it. I should have trusted your judgement. Even though I haven't seen it all, I know it's perfect for you.'

They embraced, both of them with tears in their eyes.

'The bus is here!' Ned called up the stairs.

Ned's surprise for Jonas and Rachel was two huge suites at the Blue Lagoon hotel, each with its own private little lagoon, hewn out of the lava rock, just beyond the full-height glass doors that led outside from the lounge areas. He had thought it would be fun for the hens and stags to have their own time and then to meet for dinner in the girls' suite which had the bigger lounge and a dining table.

'Ned, this is amazing,' said Rachel as they all explored the first suite together. 'This is the first place I came to when I arrived in Iceland, and I absolutely loved it.'

'I didn't know that. I just thought it would be a good place to come and relax and enjoy some time together before the big day.'

'You will come to the wedding with Anna, won't you?' Rachel asked. 'We haven't sent out any invites yet but everyone who's coming just knows.'

'I'd love that, thank you.'

'Thank you for this, it's really special.'

Ned shuffled awkwardly. 'It means a lot to me that you guys have had my back while I've been here. That doesn't happen to me very often.'

Rachel hugged him. 'Now off you go and enjoy yourself with the menfolk.'

Anna was sorry to see Ned leave with the others. Her heart was bursting with love for him, especially because of what he'd just said to Rachel.

'Come on, ladies,' said Gudrun, pulling off her clothes while they stood in the lounge. 'Let's get in!'

'Gudrun, remember that Anna and I are prudish Brits. Can't you strip off in the bedroom?'

Anna laughed and began to strip off her clothes. 'Come on Rach, you're going to be one of them soon enough. Lose your inhibitions!'

'Oooh, we could skinny dip as we have the private pool!' Gudrun was naked now and already pulling the door open, quickly closing it when a gust of icy air shot into the room.

'Gudrun, you've forgotten about the most important part of any hen night,' Anna said. 'Alcohol.'

'Ah, I think that is what this is for,' Kristen said, pulling a bottle of champagne out of a mini fridge which was cleverly camouflaged within the wall.

'Yes, Kristen! Now we can get in,' announced Anna.

Gudrun waited, naked, beside the door while they all got ready. She had poured four glasses of champagne which were waiting for them on the table, and she had quickly opened the door to put the rest of the bottle outside to keep cold.

Anna felt self-conscious but at the same time, comfortable because it was just the four of them and Gudrun and Kristen were so unfazed, it made it all seem quite normal.

They each took a glass of bubbly, then Gudrun pulled the door open, and they all squealed as the cold air hit their skin, but it was just a couple of steps across the wooden decking to the warmth of the pool. The sighs when they got in were audible and they all laughed once they were nicely submerged and taking their first sip of champagne.

'To Rachel! *Skál*!'

They clinked glasses and then relaxed back into the steamy, cloudy water.

'This is blissful,' said Anna, marvelling at how quickly she had become relaxed. 'I'd come here all the time if I lived here.'

'It is not the same if you are in the big pool with all the tourists unless it is a quiet day,' said Kristen. 'This is a treat to have a pool to ourselves.'

'Your boyfriend's brilliant, Anna,' Rachel said. 'Not that I minded going to the gin bar for my hen night, but this is another level.'

'I suppose this is normal if you are famous,' said Gudrun.

'I don't think Ned's done anything like this since he's been here, apart from our dinner in the tomato greenhouse. Maybe he does stuff like this at home, but I don't think he's that materialistic.' As she was talking, she realised that she and Ned didn't talk about that at all. They'd barely covered the topic of what his life as a famous person was like. She knew Ned here, in Iceland and because she didn't keep up with celebrity gossip like Rachel did, not much more than that.

'He's not often in the celebrity magazines unless it's for something to do with the band,' Rachel said. 'I don't think he's one of those celebrities who goes to the opening of everything.'

'That's why he's enjoyed being here so much, I think. It's the first time he's been able to have a normal life for a long time.'

'Maybe that is why he is single,' Gudrun said. 'It is hard to meet a woman who loves him not for his money.'

They could hear the whoops from next door of the men making their way into the pool. It wasn't close enough to be able to make out any conversation, which was a shame, but it was good to hear them enjoying themselves.

After a while, Anna needed to go to the loo and offered to grab more champagne on her way back and bring some towels for when everyone else got out, something they now realised they had forgotten in their hurry to get in.

The heat of the pool was quite intense so getting out wasn't as bad as getting in and Anna quite enjoyed the sensation of being cold for as long as it took her to go inside. When she looked back as she closed the door, the steam was so thick she could barely see her friends through it.

Out of habit, she checked her phone before going back outside. And wished she hadn't. After she'd sent the press statement out on Ned's behalf saying that he was in the south of France writing, she'd set up Google alerts on her phone to monitor what, if anything, was reported as a result. So far, it had been verbatim regurgitation of what she had put in the release along with a few stock photos of Ned.

But this was something else.

There was an article on a sleazy gossip website with a blurry photo of Ned playing at the open mic night. It had named the bar and said that he was in disguise and hiding in Reykjavik.

Anna's heart was palpitating. She knew what Ned's reaction would be to this, and it wouldn't be good. She was also conscious of the fact that this impacted her to some extent as well. She and Ned didn't have a plan for what was going to happen when they went back to London, but they did know they were going to be together. It was a big step for both of them to come out publicly as a couple and neither of them was ready to leave the bubble of normalness that Iceland had given Ned.

'Are you alright?' Rachel asked when Anna got back in the pool and passed a fresh bottle of champagne around.

'I just had a Google alert. I think Ned's secret is out.'

'What does that mean? You think the press will turn up?'

Anna nodded. 'Almost definitely. I should tell him, but I know he'll take it badly and I don't want him to feel that he's lost control of his life.'

'Waiting until tomorrow won't do any harm. Let him have a nice time here. No one knows where he is now. Worry about tomorrow tomorrow.'

It was good advice from Rachel, but Anna couldn't help feeling that somehow, she needed to get in front of this for Ned, on a professional level. What would she do if it was any other client? Not that she dealt much with this kind of thing, she tended to steer clear of having to manage celebrity dramas, but she'd dealt with her fair share of having to manage a situation that was seemingly out of control. That thought took her back to Freddie's wedding and the fact that the last time she'd been involved in any damage limitation, it hadn't gone that well.

'I don't think I'll tell him until I have a plan. I'll think about what to do and talk to him tomorrow.'

They managed to drag themselves out of the pool in time to dress for dinner. Ned and the others knocked on the door at seven o'clock, all in black tie, looking devilishly handsome. Brun had even tended to his unruly beard.

'You guys look amazing!' said Rachel. 'I didn't know you owned a tux, Olafur.'

'Ned organised them for us,' said Olafur, looking pleased with himself because Gudrun was barely able to conceal her feelings about how much she liked seeing him dressed up.

'It is a shame we don't have a room each,' she said with a sigh.

'He can keep the suit,' said Ned, laughing.

Anna tried to put the whole situation with the press out of her mind and concentrated on taking in the wonderful sight of Ned in a dinner jacket. His unshaven chin now looked less unkempt and more roguish, and she was thinking the same as Gudrun.

'You look like I need to take you to bed,' Anna whispered into Ned's ear, swooning even more as she breathed in his aftershave. '

'I was thinking the same thing. I might make a call, see if I get another room for us.'

Anna buried her face in his chest and shook her head.

'No, this is for Jonas and Rachel. Control yourself.'

She grinned at him, and the worry crept back into her chest as she saw the love in his eyes. It was awful. She felt like she was betraying him. But she didn't know what else to do because her biggest fear was that as soon as she told him he would want to leave. And as much as she loved him, it was too new a love to justify abandoning Rachel, so close to the wedding and just as the work Anna had done on her business was gaining traction. She couldn't start attaching her life to Ned's, not yet and not in response to something that was nothing to do with her.

The dinner was spectacularly good. A three-course feast with fabulous wine, accompanied by stories and anecdotes that only good friends would enjoy. Once they'd finished eating, they all decided to take another dip but together this time and with swimming costumes on. The men went next door to get ready.

'What an amazing night,' said Rachel as they got changed.

'It's not over yet,' Anna said, trying to sound more buoyant than she felt. She didn't want to put a damper on the night, another reason why it was better to wait until tomorrow to tell Ned, but she had a feeling of dread that she couldn't shake off.

23

The next morning, they all checked out after breakfast and Siggi drove them back to Reykjavik. A grey drizzle had settled over the city, and everyone was very quiet on the drive back, the weather reinforcing the feeling of anti-climax they all had after having had such a great time.

Ned decided to get out at Anna's house, and once they'd said their goodbyes to everyone, he carried the bags up the path while she ran ahead to open the door.

He set the bags down in the lounge, took off his glasses which had steamed up, and then pulled his coat off while Anna turned on a couple of lamps to chase away the mid-morning gloom.

'Is something on your mind?' he asked while he rubbed his glasses dry on his shirt. 'You've been quiet this morning.'

This was the moment. She was going to have to tell him.

He put his glasses back on and came over to take her in his arms.

'I've got something to tell you,' he said with a smile before he'd waited for an answer from her to his previous comment.

Anna closed her eyes and savoured the embrace, letting herself melt into him, all the time wondering whether this would be the last time things were normal between them.

She pulled away, took his hand, and led him to the sofa where they sat down next to each other. Anna shifted so she was facing him, and she could see he was expecting something bad from the look on his face.

'You know when I drafted that press release for you the other day, after you'd spoken to Freddie,' she began.

Ned nodded, his expression changing from concern to a resigned grimace. 'Something's happened. Is it out? They know where I am?'

'There's a website, a trashy one, that has pictures of you at the open mic night and they know you're here. But it's just one website, Ned.'

It was one website last night, but Anna knew it could be bigger than that by now. She hadn't checked because she didn't want to know.

'Shit,' he said, leaning back and raking his hands through his hair. 'Did it break this morning?'

'Yesterday,' she said.

'Yesterday?' He was quiet but his tone was unmistakable. 'And you waited until now to say something?' He stood up and paced across the lounge.

'We were having such a great time, it seemed a shame to worry you with it when there's nothing we can do.'

'If I'd known yesterday, I could have been on a plane yesterday, Anna. There will be press everywhere by now.'

'You don't know that. Anyway, what difference does it make if they've found out where you are? It doesn't mean you have to leave.'

Ned laughed a strange, almost mocking laugh, that told Anna he thought she knew nothing of the situation he was in.

'This is the first time in years that I've had time to myself with no one watching. And now that's over, there's no point in staying.'

Anna felt like he'd stabbed her in the heart.

Didn't he think she was worth staying for?

She could have stood in front of him and asked him why she wasn't enough of a reason to stay, but she couldn't take the risk. She'd never opened herself up to a man before, and now, the Ned she'd built a relationship with, the first proper relationship she'd ever had, he'd lost sight of her. He was spiralling in the face of a situation he thought he'd found himself in before he even knew exactly what was going on.

'Okay, so the press knows where you are, but they will know where you are if you go home to London. What's the difference?'

If he could speak to her like she was not the person he'd entangled his life with for the past few weeks, as if she was someone of no consequence at all, she could speak to him with a frankness she hadn't needed to call on since she'd been in Iceland.

'Well, it's easy to say that when you don't have that kind of problem.'

This was crazy. He was quietly erasing the bond they'd built up with every word that he uttered. Anna felt as if she needed to wake him up somehow from this nightmare he thought he was in, but she didn't think he would hear her, even if he was listening.

'I'm not pretending that I understand, Ned, but you're not in this on your own anymore.'

She knew what else she wanted to say but it really would be laying her heart on the line. Taking a deep breath, she said it anyway. What did she have to lose because she felt like he was slipping away.

'If we're going to last, you have to let me be with you on this. You're not the one dealing with it, we are. Leaving isn't the answer. We can face it together, from here. Nothing has to change.'

Ned looked at her. She couldn't read his expression and for

a few seconds thought she might have finally made him understand. But then he picked up his coat and began pulling it on.

'Where are you going?'

'I have to go. I need to pack up and leave before the place is overrun with press.'

'You don't know that'll happen. What's the harm in waiting and seeing?'

Despite her attempts to stay in control, she knew she was on the very verge of begging him to stay.

He picked up his bag and hooked it over his shoulder.

'I'm sorry, Anna.'

Now that he'd stopped, purely because he needed to say goodbye to her, she could see in his eyes that he still felt something for her. She'd thought he loved her. No, she knew that he did, and he was fighting it because something bigger had taken over and frightened him.

'Ned.' She took his hands in hers and he looked away as if looking at her would change his mind.

'I can't live like this. Not with you.'

'I love you. None of this stuff matters, you know?'

Tears were running down her face now. Had she got through to him?

'I can't deal with this and... us. I need time to work it out.'

'Don't leave.' Any thoughts of self-preservation were well and truly out of the window now. 'Let me help you.'

He shook his head and took his hands from hers.

'Anna,' he said softly, 'you can't help me. It isn't fair to drag you into this part of my life, the part that is constantly on alert. It's no way to live. I thought if I left the band, maybe things would be different for me, people would be less interested but it's always going to be like this, and I can't ask you to make that part of your life.'

'If that's what being with you means, Ned, I want that.

Don't throw this away because you're scared of how things might go. I'm tough, you don't have to worry about me or carry me. I can take care of myself, and I will take whatever comes.' And again, she put her heart right out there, 'Whatever it takes to be with you.'

Ned had tears in his eyes and Anna felt for a fleeting second that she'd changed his mind. Right up until the point that he kissed her, gently lingering on her lips, then pulled away and said, 'Bye.'

She sat back down, with her head in her hands, unable to watch him leave, unable to believe that's what he was doing.

She allowed herself a couple of sobs. Even that was more than she'd cried over anyone before, but she wasn't going to give into it. She needed a plan.

What if he got back to his apartment and no one was waiting? What if no press had bothered to come to Iceland just to track him down? After all, they knew he was here now, perhaps that was the end of it.

Anna wiped a hand across her eyes to clear them of the unshed tears that were blurring her vision and grabbed her coat from the mezzanine ladder where she'd hung it over a rung. She had to know if Ned was okay.

She locked the door and pulled her hood up against the persistent drizzle. She jogged down the path to the road, hoping to see Ned not too far ahead of her. He'd been quicker than she thought because he wasn't in sight. She carried on jogging until she could see him, he was close to home now.

Then he stopped.

Anna carried on, getting close enough to him to see why.

It was as if it happened in slow motion. Ned stopped walking just a few seconds before the pack of photographers waiting outside his apartment building noticed that he was heading their way. There was a terrific noise as they all began shouting at him at once and began to swarm towards him.

He turned back and saw her but didn't pause to acknowledge her before he headed around the side of the building to the back.

Anna had no idea whether he could get in that way and followed him, thinking bizarrely that she might be of some help if the swarm of press caught up with him. But when she turned the corner, he'd gone. Instead, the swarm was coming for her. That's what it felt like as they rushed at her but jostled and pushed past her because she wasn't who they were looking for.

In that instant, Anna was grateful that they'd never known that she was anything to do with Ned Nokes because it was terrifying. She had some insight now into how it might feel if that was coming towards you, wanting you, and she felt deep sympathy for Ned, understanding where his fear stemmed from.

But now, there was nothing else she could do but go home and hope that Ned would come to realise what he was leaving behind.

24

Ned slammed the door behind him, thankful that he'd had the foresight to scope out another entrance and exit when he'd moved in. At the time it had seemed ridiculous but was borne of the experience of many, many exits through back doors or basement kitchens of hotels, loading bays, basically any route that wasn't on the radar of a pack of paparazzi.

He'd seen Anna in the street. She must have followed him. He'd wanted to stand there, raise his hands and tell her, 'This is what I was talking about. This is what I'm trying to protect you from. This is what has driven us to this point of no return.' Now she'd seen it for herself, perhaps she'd understand.

He trudged up the stairs to his apartment, went inside and dumped his bag and coat on the nearest chair. He pulled a bottle of whisky out of the cupboard and poured himself a stiff measure, even though it was still before lunchtime.

Looking out of the window onto the street, he could see that the photographers had reassembled at the front door, probably with a few stationed around the back now that they knew that was an option for him. And now that they knew he was in there, they'd stay until he made a move.

He sat in his favourite chair and pulled it away from the

window so that he could gaze outside without anyone seeing him, his phone in his hand.

Not being in the band anymore meant that he had to go through things like this alone. Gone were the days of the four of them sitting around, watching events unfold on social media, reassuring each other, making light of seemingly serious situations with friendly banter and a few beers while their publicity teams dealt with the media frenzy for them.

And now, he was facing this by himself and was in danger of forgetting what every publicity person he'd ever worked with had drummed into him - don't look at social media.

Ned opened a new window and typed his name into Google. He'd never done it before, at least not since he was trying to make a living as a session musician while all the time hoping for his big break. Back then he'd have been thrilled to see himself at the top of a google search.

The top few results were the same story repeated almost word for word, about how he was in hiding in Reykjavik and had been spotted at a local talent show. Nice of them to call it a talent show just to make him sound desperate.

Then there was something different, around halfway down the page. It was a series of photos which had been shot in quick succession of him and Anna embracing after his set at the open mic night. And they'd picked up on the fact that she was at Freddie's wedding, showing the grainy drone shot of them standing together in the church porch. It was only a matter of time before someone worked out who she was, and they'd track her down too.

Ned threw his phone onto the sofa in frustration, then downed the rest of the whisky before heading to the kitchen to pour himself another one. He picked his phone up and called Freddie.

'Hey, Fred.'

'Ned, the man of the moment!

'For all the wrong reasons,' said Ned glumly.

'Ah, come on Neddy. All that's happened is that you've been tracked down. It was bound to happen sooner or later. You had a good run of it.'

It was true. A few weeks of being incognito would have been unthinkable when he'd been a member of the band.

'I'm just bitter because I'm not ready to come home. It was brilliant and I wanted it to end on my terms, not the bloody media's.'

'Can't you stick it out? They'll lose interest pretty quickly now they've got what they wanted.'

That might have been true a few weeks ago but now he had other people to consider.

'It's Anna. They'll come for her and I can't put her through that, it's not fair. She came here the same as me, to escape from whatever shit was going on in her life and the last thing she needs is me bringing all that drama for her. It isn't fair.'

'So, what's the plan? You're leaving her there?'

'Yes, she has her friend's wedding in a couple of weeks, so she'd want to stay. I've told her I'm leaving, it's the only option. I'm not going to have the peace to write or the freedom to play at the open mic night anymore so there's no point staying.'

'And she understands?'

He wasn't sure he had fully explained himself in his haste to get away, but she'd seen with her own eyes what he was up against.

'She saw me being chased down the street by a pack of paps, so I guess so. Look, is there any chance I can arrange a plane on the band's account?'

'Sure, whatever you need, man.'

'Thanks.' It felt good to know he could get away without having to run the gauntlet at the airport.

'Look, Ned. Don't let this get to you. Leaving the band

means there's interest in what you do next, that's all this is. It's not how it'll be. You'll be the master in the end, you know that right?'

Ned needed to hear Freddie's reassuring tone. Leaving the band had been a big decision and Ned thought he'd thought it through - he had thought it through, just not every part of it. Having to deal with this kind of thing alone was making him a little bit paranoid and he was in danger of losing sight of the bigger picture.

'Thanks, Fred, I needed that.'

'Anytime, man. You know that. Even if you're not in the band anymore, you're always in the band.'

Ned finished the call, promising Freddie that he would call as soon as he was back in London, then he finished his drink and headed to the bedroom to pack.

His phone buzzed with a call from Brun.

'Hey, Brun.'

'Anna called and said there are press people outside your building.'

Ned briefly wondered why Anna had felt the need to share that with Brun.

'Yes, there's quite the throng.'

'Do you need some help?'

'Unless you can do something to entice them elsewhere, I'm not sure there's much you can do but I appreciate the offer.'

'When do you need to leave?'

Ned outlined his plan with Brun who promised that by the time Ned was ready to leave there would be no press to deal with.

As good as his word, about ten minutes before the car was due to arrive to take him to the city airport, the crowd outside the building began to disperse. Ned stood watching, grinning as whatever Brun had planned seemed to be working like a charm.

Just as he watched the last few follow the pack to wherever they were going, he saw the car he had booked pull up.

This was it. Time to go.

It was such a sudden ending and he realised he wasn't ready. Was he making a mistake leaving in such a hurry? Leaving Anna behind? That morning he had thought he had it all and now it was just him, alone again.

But he couldn't stay. Not now. He gathered up his bags and turned to take a last look at the place he had called home for the past few weeks. It had started to feel like home, but Ned knew that wasn't about the apartment, but about the life he'd started to carve out for himself here. He'd been naive to think that things could continue forever, that his life would remain uninterrupted by the outside world. Leaving was the right decision. It was time to go back to London and start his new life properly.

Ned sighed with relief once he was in the car and on the way to the airport. The blacked-out windows reassured him that he'd make it to the private jet without any hindrance. He pulled his phone out and sent a text to Brun, aside from saying thank you, to find out what he'd done to entice the paps from outside his front door.

I told one of them that there are underground tunnels linking all the buildings and that I'd seen you down at the bar in the harbour.

He'd added a laughing-crying-face emoji and Ned chuckled, knowing that Brun had probably enjoyed that.

He clicked off Brun's message and clicked onto the thread he had with Anna. He already regretted the way he'd left things. Now that he was out of the situation, he could see more clearly that he had left things badly. He'd run away from her when none of this was anything to do with her and he was beginning to wish that she'd tried harder to make him stay and talk to her. But he knew he wouldn't have listened. That kind of situation with the press just made everything seem very hazy as if his brain was full of fog.

I'm sorry. I'll call you when I get back to London.

That was all he could say. He hoped that whatever they'd started could survive outside of Reykjavik, especially now when it had quite possibly already foundered.

25

Anna read the text from Ned. It wasn't what she'd hoped for but at least he had said sorry. He should be sorry. But that didn't help her to understand. where she stood now. She was still finding it hard to believe what had happened. Ned had run away because some press people had turned up on his doorstep. Wasn't he used to that kind of thing? It was hard to believe that alone had freaked him out enough to leave when he must have come across that sort of attention - and more - when he was in The Rush.

It seemed as if there had to be more to it than that. Okay, he'd been angry that she hadn't told him when she'd seen the google alert the day before but perhaps he'd come to realise that it was getting too serious between them, that he wasn't ready to have a relationship and certainly not ready to have the press know that he was with her. She wasn't the kind of woman someone like him would date, she'd always known that, but it had been easy to disregard that fact when she was with him, having him adore her, write songs about her. Love her.

There was a knock at the door and Rachel came into the house.

'Hey, Jonas said Ned's left? Is that true?' She looked

puzzled, as well she might.

'Yes, he's gone.'

'But...'

Anna shrugged. 'I know.'

Then Rachel took charge, insisted Anna put her coat on and marched them down to the seafront. They didn't talk on the way but once they were sat on a slightly damp bench, overlooking the grey, choppy sea, Anna told Rachel everything.

'I suppose it's hard for us to know what it's like to have that kind of press attention,' Rachel said.

'But it must be like that all the time for him, why was he so freaked out that he left?'

'Have you tried to talk to him?'

'No, I don't know what to say, Rach. I thought he'd ask me to go with him. I thought he loved me.'

Anna's face crumpled and she buried her face in her woolly-gloved hands.

Rachel put an arm across her shoulders and pulled her into a hug.

'He loves you, Anna, I'm sure of it. It's just a blip. He's never had a serious relationship, perhaps he just got scared?'

Anna sniffed and nodded. 'I thought that. But how can I be with someone who runs at the first sign of trouble? It's not even anything that bad and he's gone. What does that mean for us, is he going to sod off every time something difficult happens?'

'I don't know but you need to talk to him. See if he'll come back for the wedding? Things might have died down by then and he might feel differently.'

'About what?'

Rachel laughed. 'I don't know, I'm just trying to be helpful. Who knows what goes on in his head, Anna. If you don't know, I definitely don't. Jonas is a lot more straightforward.'

'Thanks for coming round, I needed that.'

'So now that you owe me, do you want to go for coffee or cocktails?'

'I think coffee might be the safer option. A couple of cocktails might turn into drowning my sorrows and I don't want to go down that road.'

'Coffee it is. Oh, in better news, I've filled all the slots I set aside for tour companies to book with me. I had a couple more emails this morning.'

'That's amazing, Rach. Perhaps we should do cocktails after all.'

'And also, Jonas is at the estate agents now because we think we've sold the house.'

'Already? I haven't even shown anyone round yet.'

'It's some friend of Jonas's so they've seen it before and just want to do the deal as soon as we can.'

'I'm happy to stay in a hotel until the wedding, you know that.'

Rachel shook her head. 'There's no way it'll get sorted until after that anyway so stay there until you go back to London.'

They walked to Te & Kaffi, a couple of doors down from Snug and saw Gudrun rearranging something in the window as they passed. She spotted them and gestured for them to go inside.

'Rachel, the candles have arrived! And Olafur had a text to say that the beer is ready, so he has gone to collect it this afternoon.'

'Beer?' Anna asked. She didn't remember that being on the wedding to-do list.

'Olafur has a friend who brews beer and is doing special wedding beer with labels and everything for the party,' Gudrun explained, perching on the arm of the sofa that was in the window.

'Oh, that's cool,' said Anna, feeling quite excited about the wedding now that it was so close.

The reception was being held at a barbecue restaurant, somewhere in the Golden Circle which was just outside Reykjavik and where all the most popular tourist attractions were, like the geyser and the place where the continents of Europe and Northern America met, and you could walk between them. It was one of Jonas's most popular tours and one that Rachel had been on back in the Spring. This barbecue place was somewhere that meant something to her and Jonas and although it was a risk that by the time the wedding rolled around in November, snow could hamper their guests getting to and from it, they felt it was perfect. And beer was the perfect accompaniment.

'Is Ned coming back for the wedding?' Gudrun asked because of course, Anna realised, she already knew from Olafur, via Brun, that Ned had left.

'I hope so.'

'Rachel, come and see the candles,' Gudrun said excitedly.'

'I won't be a sec,' said Rachel and the two of them disappeared downstairs.

Anna, deciding she didn't care whether she was part of the window display or not, sat on the sofa and pulled out her phone. It was still too soon to call him, but she was feeling desperate to find out whether Ned leaving meant that he had left her or whether he was expecting that they could pick up where they left off when she got back to London.

London. In a couple of weeks, the wedding would be over, Rachel would be married, and the only option was to go back. She'd hardly given any thought to as to what she was going to do. It still felt too soon for any PR agency worth its salt to want her but that was all she knew.

She mindlessly scrolled through Twitter just for something to do while Rachel was still downstairs looking at candles.

Seeing something familiar she stopped herself and scrolled back. It was a tweet about the open mic night with a picture of Ned. They were advertising that Eddie was playing that evening. It had obviously not crossed Ned's mind to let them know that he wasn't going to be there. In his defence, as far as Anna was aware, all he had said was, 'see you next week,' to the compere but it had been taken literally.

Later that evening, Anna strolled down to the bar by herself intending to catch the guy who organised the running order before anything got started so he'd know not to expect Ned.

'Hi,' she said to the usual guy behind the bar who greeted her with a friendly smile.

'Hello, is Eddie with you?'

'No, actually, I came to tell you he can't make it tonight.'

'Ah, that is a shame. He is the best guy we have had for ages. I was hoping to talk to him about working together.'

'Oh, are you a musician too?'

He laughed and shook his head. 'No, no! I am an agent and a publicist for musicians. The open mic night is a good way for me to find new talented people and help them out at the beginning of their career.'

'Well, you have a good eye for it.'

He looked puzzled.

'He used to be in The Rush.'

The guy's eyes widened in realisation. 'He is Ned Nokes.'

Anna nodded.

'Does he have an agent?' The guy said, with a huge belly laugh.

'I don't think so,' said Anna.

He grinned, shaking his head. 'He is out of my league anyway. Good luck to him. He was wasted in that band.'

Anna walked home, thinking about what the man in the bar had said. He was using the open mic night to find clients for himself. Perhaps there was something in that. Not that she knew anything about music, but she knew whether she liked something or not, maybe that was enough?

Her initial excitement about it diminished pretty quickly once she thought about it a bit harder and realised that she knew very little about being an agent or promoter in the music business. The few times that she'd dealt with anyone in that kind of role, it had seemed like a very closed shop. You had to know people who knew people. Whoever heard of an agent who had started from nowhere with no contacts in the music industry? It was crazy.

But the idea kept niggling away at her and she knew she had to at least give it proper consideration before she could let it go. She got back to the house, locked the door behind her and went straight to the kitchen to open a bottle of wine. She sat on the sofa, opened up her laptop and began googling for open mic nights around the area of London where she lived, in Soho.

There were a few listed but they seemed to be mainly for blues music. Anna wasn't sure what genre Ned would describe his music as, but it wasn't blues. Maybe there was a gap in the market. If she could start something that was like this one in Reykjavik, she was sure people would love it.

She picked up her phone.

Are you home?

If it wasn't for the fact that she was keen to hear his thoughts on her idea, she might not have made contact first. She felt strongly that he owed her an apology. A better one than the text he'd sent.

She watched the three dots pulsing as he replied.

I'll call you.

Her phone sprang into life with a FaceTime call.

Ned appeared with a sheepish smile on his face.

'Hey,' he said.

'Good trip?' Anna asked, not caring that much but not knowing what else to say for the moment.

'Yes, it's weird to be home.' He looked around him as if he was assessing wherever it was he was sitting.

'I went to the bar today and let them know you wouldn't be playing tonight.'

'Thanks.' He bowed his head and rubbed his palm across his forehead before letting out a sigh. 'You didn't have to do that.'

'Well, they sent out a tweet about Eddie, so I thought they ought to know.'

He looked right into the camera now, his eyes tired behind his glasses. 'I'm so sorry, Anna. I never meant to leave like that. To leave you.'

'But you did. And now what? I don't know what we have now, whether we have anything.'

'Me leaving is nothing to do with us. I feel the same way as I did before. Yes, I was annoyed that you didn't give me the head's up about that story being out, but it doesn't change anything.'

Anna couldn't take in what he was saying because everything had changed. Their whole existence together had been in Reykjavik and now he was gone.

'Look, I realise that you have a very different life from me but I'm shocked that this press attention affected you like this. It can't have been the worst thing that's happened to you over the years, surely?'

He shrugged. 'I know I overreacted, and I think it's because it's the first time I've been by myself, not with the band. It made me feel more exposed and kind of threatened. I loved being in Iceland with no one knowing and it was just such a shock to realise that was over.'

Anna was beginning to understand. Ned was struggling with his new life, not having his friends to turn to at moments like this must be hard.

'Okay, well let's call it evens then.'

'Deal,' he said smiling. 'So, are you going to the open mic night?'

'No, but I have an idea and I'd love to see what you think.'

She explained to him about the way the guy at the bar used the night to spot new talent and then helped the acts get a head start. Ned nodded and smiled as she spoke, she could tell he thought it had legs before he even said anything.

'It's a great idea, I'd love to help you get started. Once you've found a venue, maybe Eddie could play your first one?'

She laughed. 'Eddie could but I think Ned Nokes might blow people's minds too quickly.'

'Point taken. I have a couple of indie record labels who might be able to send some of their up-and-coming artists to fill some of your slots until you get established.'

'That'd be great, thank you.'

A gentle silence settled between them.

'I miss you.'

'Will you come back for the wedding?' She felt brave asking but given that he seemed to admit that he'd left in haste, perhaps it wasn't too much to hope for.

'Yes. If you'll have me.'

26

Anna was waiting in the arrival's hall at Keflavik airport. Ned had come to terms with the fact that as a solo artist it wasn't all that viable to travel alone by private plane and instead was opting for first-class travel on a normal flight. It did mean that he could bypass the public areas at London Heathrow, but Keflavik was too small for that, so Anna was his welcoming party and she had borrowed Jonas's Jeep for the occasion.

Since Ned had left, they had spoken every day. It had begun with tentative conversations, each of them gauging where they stood. Now that they found themselves in the position of knowing that they wanted a relationship with each other, they were still overcoming the hurdles of how that might look in reality. Anna knew that the time apart had given Ned some clarity on what he wanted. The break in Iceland had been an amazing way for him to decompress after leaving the band and although it had ended abruptly, it was never going to be anything more than an extended holiday, and he realised that now. It had also given Anna time to focus on what she was going to do next and now that she had turned her idea into a more solid plan, she was keen to get back to London after the wedding and put it into action.

She'd made some enquiries at a couple of pubs that would be promising venues and had also been in touch with the indie record labels that Ned had suggested and felt that she had something she could start to build on. One thing she was sure of was that she was no longer interested in going back to the career she'd had before, even if that had been an option. She was looking forward to seeing Ned as much for the opportunity to discuss her plans as for anything else.

In her hands she held a sign with his name on it that she'd drawn out that morning but now that she was surrounded by strangers, she felt like a fan of The Rush, standing there with a sign that said Ned Nokes. Then she smiled, headed to a nearby hire car company's desk and asked to borrow a pen then spent a couple of minutes writing Eddie on the back of her sign. She wrote it in bubble writing and decorated it with plenty of hearts which she knew would make him laugh.

Back at the arrivals exit, she knew he would be out any minute once a fresh stream of people began to emerge from the latest flight. Her heart was beating hard. She was so looking forward to seeing him but even though they had got past the circumstances of his leaving before, she was a little bit nervous about seeing him in the flesh again.

He came through, carrying a big holdall and had a huge smile on his face once he spotted her sign. He'd had a haircut since the last time they'd done a video call, but he was still wearing his glasses. He still looked like her Ned more than Ned Nokes.

There was an unspoken understanding that no public displays of affection would happen. Anna squashed the feeling that made her want to throw her arms around him and give him a big kiss right in the middle of the arrivals hall and instead beamed her biggest smile and squeezed his hand, knowing that once they got home, she wouldn't have to hold herself back anymore.

As they walked outside, both unaware of how cold it was, bathed as they were in each other's gaze, Anna felt her heart gently expanding as if someone was blowing it up like a balloon. Ned was the one. She knew that, right now, at this moment. Everything was perfect.

She drove back to town, leaving the Jeep parked in a convenient spot for Jonas to pick it up when he wanted to. Ned followed her up the cobbled path to the house, the fences and trees in the tiny gardens still all festooned with twinkling fairy lights as if it were Christmas.

'Welcome back,' said Anna, wrapping her arms around his neck and pulling him towards her as soon as they had closed the door. Ned dropped his bag on the floor and picked her up, carrying her the short distance to the sofa before laying her down gently and continuing his kisses before she stopped him.

'I need to take my coat off.'

Ned laughed and took his coat off, throwing it over the nearby chair before helping Anna with hers.

'I missed you so much, Anna. I was an idiot to leave. What was I thinking?' He breathed the words into her ear as he ran his hands under her layers of clothing, finding the curve of her breast with his fingers.

After a few more minutes, Anna suggested moving to the bedroom. Although they had to break apart to climb the ladder up to the mezzanine, it didn't spoil the moment.

Later on, still wrapped in each other's arms as if they were each afraid to let the other go after being apart for a couple of weeks, Ned asked Anna if she was enjoying living in the little house.

'I love it, it's so cosy. I'm glad you're staying with me this time.'

'Me too. Although technically, you're staying with me.'

Anna frowned. 'What do you mean?'

'This is my place. I bought it,' he said easily as if it were the most normal thing in the world. 'I tried to tell you that last morning, but you got in there first.'

Anna struggled to remember anything about that morning apart from the argument they'd had before Ned left. 'Did you? But Rachel and Jonas would have said.'

'They didn't know. I asked my people to keep it quiet.'

'But why?'

Ned shifted until he was lying on his side, looking into her eyes. 'Because I love it here. It's the first place I'd ever stayed that felt more like home than home. I know now that might have been more to do with you being here than anything else but still, it's a solid investment.'

'I can't believe you just bought a house somewhere you don't even live.' Anna let out a small laugh of disbelief. 'That's a definite pop star thing to do.'

Ned answered her by digging his fingers into her waist, in a playful tickle, making her squeal. 'Well, I am a pop star,' he said with a glint in his eye.

Anna tried to tickle him back, but he grabbed her wrists in one hand, sending her into hysterical laughter when he carried on tickling that spot just above her collarbone.

'I give in!' she shouted. Then once he'd stopped, she hooked her legs around his and manoeuvred herself on top of him. Now she was in charge.

That evening, when they finally made it out of bed again, they ordered a takeaway and sat on the sofa with it on their laps, sharing a bottle of red wine.

'How's the open mic thing going?' Ned asked between mouthfuls of noodles.

'I've booked a venue and made a Facebook page which has had a few shares so I'm hoping word will spread.'

'That's brilliant. The offer's still open if you want Eddie to play on your opening night.'

'Thanks. I'll see how it goes before I commit.'

Ned nodded thoughtfully. 'And so you should. You don't want Eddie stealing a spot from a talented newcomer.'

'I went to see Thor again. He runs the open mic night here,' she added when Ned looked bemused as to who Thor was. 'He said I could use the photos I took here for my Facebook page. He gets everyone to sign a waiver to say they permit the use of photos or whatever. Did you sign that?'

Ned nodded. 'Yeah, it was pretty harmless, and I still don't think most people realised it was me and if they did, they didn't care that much. It's a good idea. Gives you free publicity material. That's nice of him to let you use the photos.'

'He knows I'm friends with Eddie. I think that's what swung it,' Anna said, smiling.

'Eddie's amazing.'

'Steady. We don't want Eddie getting too big for his boots.'

Anna took the plates and headed into the kitchen with them. Ned followed with the wine glasses, topping them up from the bottle on the kitchen table.

'Do you think you'll do anything to the house?' Anna asked as she rinsed the plates under the tap.

'I don't think so. It's cosy, that's the main thing. I don't think anything needs doing really. Do you?'

'No, I like it the way it is.'

'I think I'll just kit it out with some stuff so that whenever we're here we don't need to bring much with us.'

There was a lot to take in from that sentence. First, Ned was assuming that they would be here together when only two weeks ago he'd walked out of the very same front door, leaving her with little forethought or explanation. Surely it was too soon to go from that to this being their house. And not only that, their holiday house. What did that mean for everything else?

'Don't overthink that.'

Her expression must have given her away.

'It wasn't a veiled invitation to live together, Anna. It was just an assumption that we might want to come on holiday here again. Together. What harm is there in having say, an Icelandic standard winter coat and some boots in that cupboard?' He pointed to the empty kitchen cupboard that used to house Jonas's huge collection of outdoor wear. 'Don't read too much into it,' he said gently. 'Let's just enjoy it.'

'Enjoy it because it's not serious?' She was being argumentative, but she needed to flesh out what his intentions were. She wasn't prepared to live at the whim of someone else's notions and the morning that Ned had left was now flashing like a series of photographs through her mind. How it had made her feel, how all the love she'd thought was there between them had disappeared in that instant that he heard about the google alert.

Ned sighed. 'Enjoying something doesn't mean it isn't serious. I'm as serious about you as it's possible to be.' He came towards her, taking her hands in his. His eyes were full of sincerity. 'Me leaving… I know that was a crazy reaction. I won't do that again. We're in this together. You can trust me.'

Anna couldn't help but be hypnotised by his reassuring tone and the look in his eyes. She wanted to believe him more than anything and there was nothing to stop her. So, he'd made a mistake. He'd spent the last ten years in a world where he could trust very few people and that was not something that was going to change instantly. It would take time for both of them to learn to navigate that as a couple. But she knew she wanted to try. And if she was going to follow her heart for the first time in her life, she needed to stop allowing anything to hold her back.

27

Everyone had been bussed into the reception venue that afternoon in preparation for the wedding which was taking place at dusk. Jonas and his friends had managed to hire several nearby holiday cabins from family and friends so that all the guests had somewhere convenient to stay, as there were no hotels this far from the city.

Gudrun was in charge of corralling the guests for the wedding and had many lists which she carried in an unorganised looking sheaf of paper that she was constantly referring to. Now, everyone was standing outside the restaurant waiting for their next instruction.

'Alan and Mary, you are in the cabin over there, number four,' she called.

'Say something, Alan, we need the key and goodness knows how we'll walk all that way in the snow with these bags,' said Rachel's mum.

Anna had volunteered Ned to be the escort for Mary while Alan was doing his duties as father-of-the-bride but had yet to introduce them. It seemed like a good time now.

'Don't worry, Mary. Me and Ned can help you take your things to the cabin.'

Mary turned around and her face softened as soon as she

realised it was Anna.

'Lovely to see you, Anna,' she said, pulling her in for a kiss on the cheek. 'And this is your young man?'

'I'm Ned, Mrs Richards, Mr Richards, great to meet you.' Ned shook Alan's hand and gave Mary a quick kiss which made her blush.

'It's so nice to see you girls settled, isn't it Alan?'

Alan nodded and picked up a couple of their bags, Ned took the others, and they made their way over to the nearest cluster of three cabins.

'I don't know about this wedding, Anna. It's very odd. I don't know why Rachel didn't want that lovely church in the middle of town. We could have stayed in a hotel, and it would have been much more civilised.'

Anna grinned. She loved Mary.

'It's a bit different,' she agreed, 'but that's them, isn't it? And I think it'll be beautiful, Mary.'

'Well, Jonas is a sensible lad and knows what he's doing. I suppose we have to trust him, don't we?' she said, implying that the whole affair was Jonas's idea when he'd been trying to persuade Rachel to go for something less logistically challenging just in case the weather wasn't on their side. As it was, it was a bright, clear day with the temperature hovering around six degrees Celsius. There was a bit of lying snow, enough to make things look pretty but not enough to cause any problems.

'Here we are.' Ned opened the door to the cabin which was basically one room with a tiny bathroom off the hallway, a small kitchen along one side of the room, a sofa which was piled with fresh linen and blankets and a view out of the large windows across the lake.

'Well, this is very cosy, isn't it Alan? Thank you, Ned.' she added as he put the rest of the bags down.

'Shall we help you get the bed set up?' Anna asked.

'That would be wonderful. These sofa beds have a mind of their own,' said Mary, gratefully.

Once the bed was out and made and Ned had started a fire in the stove, they said their goodbyes.

'So, I'll be back to collect you at four o'clock, Mrs Richards,' said Ned.

'Please call me Mary. Thank you, Ned, I'll be ready at four.'

'What's the next job?' Ned asked as they walked back to the restaurant hand in hand.

'I've got to help get the tables ready and I've volunteered you to help the boys with something at the wedding venue.'

'Intriguing. Okay, I'll see you later.' He kissed her before heading over to where Brun, Olafur and Siggi were gathered around a Jeep.

'Cabin number two!' she called after him.

He turned around and gave her a thumbs up, followed by blowing her a kiss.

'You are far too happy,' said Gudrun coming up behind her. 'Come with me and I will find some jobs to bring you back to earth.'

Anna linked her arm into Gudrun's. 'This day is going to be amazing.'

At just before four o'clock, Ned was ready to leave. He looked so handsome in his suit, even with the lambswool jumper he was wearing underneath his jacket. Anna was sorry they weren't going to be together until later. His hair was swept back making him look very suave, and his beard was now a very sexy-looking stubble.

'You look beautiful,' he said to her while she was still gazing at him appreciatively.

'Thanks. Make the most of this moment because I might freeze to death later without a coat on.'

The bridesmaids' dresses that she and Gudrun were wearing were long with tiered skirts which meant that they could wear leggings underneath. They were midnight blue with tiny gold dots all over them, making them look quite celestial. The tops of the dresses did have long sleeves but wearing a thermal vest underneath didn't work because the neckline was too low. They were both wearing black boots and had small golden tiaras with tiny stars that shot out in all directions off thin wires, something Rachel had commissioned from one of her local artist contacts.

Ned pulled her towards him. 'I don't think I've ever seen you look so amazing,' he said, his lips almost touching hers.

'Don't be late for Mary,' she whispered, because even though she fancied the pants off him there were things to do. This had to wait until later. He laughed. 'I wouldn't dare be late for Mary. Okay, I'm going. Have a wonderful wedding, Anna.'

Anna pulled her coat on and left the cabin just after Ned, heading to the restaurant where she was meeting Rachel, Alan and Gudrun.

The four of them were the last to leave on a minibus, having watched all the other guests leave in batches over the past half an hour or so. Darkness was beginning to fall in the slow way that it did in Iceland, and it had begun to snow very gently.

Rachel looked serene, not nervous at all, as her dad helped her out of the minibus.

'You're wearing Converse!' said Anna, catching a glimpse of her feet in a fresh pair of white boots.

'Comfy feet are everything, Anna, you know that,' she laughed.

Rachel handed her small bouquet of wildflowers to Alan while she unzipped her coat, revealing the dress that Anna had seen the tiniest peek of before.

It was stunning. The lace on the arms was beautiful but hadn't given a clue as to how amazing the rest of the dress was. The bodice was plain, with tiny stitches making a neatly fitting top with a wide neckline that showed off Rachel's décolletage to perfection. The slight fuzz of the wool made the edges look like mist where it met her skin. The skirt flowed out from the waist in larger stitches which made the fabric drape and was studded with tiny golden beads, tying the whole thing into the dresses that Gudrun and Anna wore, and the hem was a beautiful open lace pattern that grazed the ground behind Rachel when she walked. Her tiara was a larger version of the ones her bridesmaids were wearing.

'Oh, Rach, you look… amazing, absolutely perfect,' said Anna, with tears in her eyes.

'Ready, love?' Alan asked his daughter.

Rachel nodded and he took her hand and tucked it into the crook of his arm, looking like the proudest dad in the world.

Gudrun and Anna led the way towards the top of the aisle. The wedding was taking place outside a tiny chapel which was in the middle of nowhere. It was far too small to hold even the forty or so guests that they had, so the plan had always been to be outside but if the weather had been fierce, they could have all huddled inside at a push.

The chairs were facing the church and the front of it had been festooned with fairy lights. At the end of each row of chairs were small braziers, flaming to warm the guests and lend some light to the dusk. At the front, where Jonas and Olafur stood waiting were two huge braziers on either side of the doorway to the little church. The whole thing had a magical feel.

The music started and Anna and Gudrun walked down the aisle, the guests turning to look at them. Ned caught Anna's eye and winked at her. She felt overwhelmed with love for him. It was amazing to have him here with her on such a special occasion.

Anna and Gudrun stood on the other side of the aisle from

Jonas and Olafur. Jonas had turned to watch Rachel walk down the aisle. Anna could tell the exact moment that he caught sight of her because his face turned into a picture of love and awe for the woman he loved, walking toward him.

The guests cheered when the celebrant announced them as husband and wife and carried on cheering and applauding while Jonas theatrically dipped Rachel down, holding her back with just one hand while he kissed her until she wrapped her arms around his neck for fear of falling onto the snow. When they turned to face their guests, their happiness on show for all to see, everyone left their chairs and joined them at the front where Siggi and Brun magicked cups of steaming mulled wine from inside the church and began passing them around. Guests huddled around the braziers, sipping wine while Rachel and Jonas mingled amongst everyone. Olafur thoughtfully collected the coats from the minibus for the bridesmaids and Rachel, although she declined hers saying she wasn't cold and instead stayed warm by nestling into Jonas.

The minibuses began ferrying people back to the restaurant. Jonas and Rachel were the last to arrive, their guests lining the doorway and cheering as they made their way inside. Now that darkness had fallen, the place was transformed. What had seemed like a stark, run-of-the-mill restaurant by day, was now cosy and welcoming. The fire had been lit in the huge pit in the centre of the room underneath a huge chimney canopy and the beautiful candles that Gudrun had sourced were lit on each of the tables.

The staff began handing out bottles of cold wedding beer to everyone but there were bottles of wine on the tables as well. Plates of raw meat were delivered onto the tables and people began taking a seat around the fire and skewering their meat, chatting as they cooked. It was an incredible atmosphere and Anna could see why Rachel loved this place.

Ned came over to her with a plate of meat in his hand.

'Shall we?' he asked, holding out his hand and leading her around the fire to where there was a free bench that they could squat on.

'This is so cool,' he said as he prepared the meat for cooking. 'I've got no idea what any of this is, but it smells amazing in here.'

The man who was in charge of the fire raked some hot coals to the spot where they were about to cook. Ned thanked him and held his skewers over the heat.

Anna watched him, thinking how easy it was to be with him. This was how life could be for them now. After today, seeing her best friend marry the love of her life, Anna was more confident that she could have that with Ned. There was no need to hold back. If she loved him, she should let herself give into that. He was the only person she had loved like this, and she had to allow herself to be swept away because she had a feeling that if she didn't, she would never get the same chance again. Feeling so deeply about Ned had taken her by surprise and although she wasn't sure exactly how to navigate a relationship with someone she loved who loved her just as much, she knew there was no other option but to open her heart completely.

28

Ned couldn't remember a time when he'd felt so relaxed at a wedding. Or any other big event for that matter. It was so informal compared to Freddie's wedding which now that he thought about it was more of a show for other people rather than a day that reflected the love of the two people it was for. Jonas and Rachel had shared their love for each other with everyone by creating a day that was full of unpretentious ease where everyone could celebrate without the constraints of etiquette or tradition.

They'd all eaten the incredible feast that they'd cooked themselves and now everyone was waiting for the dancing to begin. A space was cleared of tables and chairs and once the music started, Jonas and Rachel began slow dancing together to the first song.

Ned felt Anna slip her hand into his as they watched. He looked down at her and found her looking at him with a look of such devotion, that he thought his heart would explode. Coming back to Iceland for this was the best decision he'd ever made. It was just what they both needed to reset things between them properly.

Everyone clapped at the end of the song and then the music changed to something more upbeat, and everyone took to the floor as well. Gudrun came over to grab Anna for a bridesmaids and bride dance and Ned watched her shoot him a reluctant smile as she went off with them.

Ned watched Mary force Alan up for a dance and smiled when they launched into some well-practised rock-and-roll steps.

His phone buzzed in his pocket, and he pulled it out to find that Freddie was calling him. He headed outside, forgetting to take his coat and instantly wrapped his arms around himself, tucking his hands into his armpits against the cold while holding his phone between his ear and his shoulder.

'Hey, Fred. How's it going?'

'Um, yeah, good, good.' Freddie was keen to get past the pleasantries.

'What's up?'

'I take it you're back with Anna?'

'Well, yes, that's why I'm here,' he said with a puzzled laugh. He'd thought Freddie had realised that he and Anna were serious.

'Something's come up. Sophia found out that Anna is the one who leaked our wedding location to the press.'

'What? No, that can't be right, Fred. She was working for the photographer at your wedding, why would she sabotage her own people?'

'Look, I don't know what to tell you. She worked for a PR agency that set up the deal for us with Hey! and they've sacked her over it.'

Ned was stunned enough to need to sit down on a wooden bench, despite it having a smattering of snowflakes over it.

'Sophia's got the wrong end of the stick.'

'I'm sorry but they're not going to fire her unless they have proof, are they? It's ruined her career from what Sophia says.'

Ned hung up in a daze. It made sense because Anna had

lost her job, hadn't she? She was taking time out to decide what to do next. Her setting up this open mic night PR thing for musicians, was that because she'd been ostracised from the industry she'd worked in before?

But at the same time, it made no sense. Why would Anna sabotage Freddie's wedding? Surely there was nothing in it for her. Ned knew her and she wasn't malicious at all. She wouldn't do anything like that.

After a few minutes of staring into the darkness, Ned realised his bottom was so cold he could no longer feel it and rose to his feet with a sigh. Things had just got back to normal and now it was all up in the air again. He wanted to believe that Anna wouldn't have done that, but Freddie had seemed so sure and what he said did fit with Anna being here and planning a new business. He was going to have to talk to her to get to the bottom of it. Ignoring it was tempting because he didn't believe it could be true but when they got back to London, it was sure to create a problem with Freddie and Sophia. At the end of the day, Freddie was his best friend, and he couldn't let that happen. He needed Freddie and Anna to love each other for his life to work.

Ned blew on his fingers which were beginning to go numb and went back inside. He headed straight for the fire pit, sat down and warmed his hands over the dying embers.

Brun wandered over with a couple of beers and offered one to Ned.

'Everything okay? You do not look as happy as you did before you went outside.'

Ned took a slug of the beer and shook his head. 'I don't know. My friend just called with some weird news.'

'Ah. Weird bad news,' said Brun knowingly.

'Yes. Pretty bad. I need to talk to Anna, but I don't want to spoil today for her.'

'It can wait?'

'I guess it can wait.'

But Ned knew that it was going to eat at him until he spoke to Anna about it. The details from the call with Freddie were buzzing around his head and he was having trouble bringing himself back into the moment. He wouldn't bring it up today but as soon as the opportunity presented itself, he'd have to.

The rest of the evening was difficult. Ned had never been very good at putting something aside to deal with later. When he'd been in the band, there was never anything to be gained from letting anything fester. Whether it was a disagreement between him and the lads or something they had to deal with together, something similar to this, it needed dealing with straight away.   He watched Anna dancing, then she spotted him and beckoned him onto the dance floor. He managed a smile but shook his head, holding his beer bottle aloft in explanation that he was finishing his drink. She blew him a kiss and carried on dancing.

It simply couldn't be true. He knew Anna. She wasn't materialistic so he doubted she would have sold Freddie and Sophia out for money. That wasn't what made her tick. And she wasn't vindictive. In all the time he'd known her she'd never once said anything bad about anyone so it seemed unlikely that she would have any kind of grudge against Freddie or Sophia. What had happened was the behaviour of a disgruntled fan or something like that. It couldn't have been Anna. There was some kind of massive misunderstanding going on.

Feeling better about the whole thing, having talked himself around to being on Anna's side, he slowly managed to put it to the back of his mind and joined her on the dance floor. She was so smiley and joyous that it helped him to forget the conversation with Freddie and he soon found himself twirling her around and dipping her, making her laugh and throw her arms around him. He hugged her to him, thinking that losing her would be the worst thing that could happen to him. This was what he wanted. He wanted her. This beautiful, smiling, happy woman who was in his arms.

It wasn't long before the music turned slower, and he and Anna folded themselves around each other and swayed.

'Ned, Anna, we're off, leave you young ones to see the night out. Thank you for everything, both of you.' Mary had no qualms about interrupting an intimate moment but neither of them minded. Anna kissed Mary's cheek while Ned shook Alan's hand, then they swapped over, and all said good night to each other.

When the music finished, everyone pulled on their coats and headed outside to a veranda which overlooked the lake. The water glistened through the inky darkness where it caught the light of the flames that were burning in the braziers set at intervals along the back of the building. There were mugs of hot chocolate for everyone and someone shouted that the aurora forecast was good.

'Hey, you two,' said Rachel, coming to join them, finally having succumbed to covering her beautiful dress with a coat.

'It's been an amazing day,' Ned said to her. 'Thanks for having me.'

'You earned your place by looking after my mum,' she said with a laugh. 'She loves you two together, reckons you'll be next.'

Anna blushed, surprising Ned who didn't think anything would throw her off, but he loved it and teased her by saying, 'Yes, this time next year…'

'Ned!' she said, blushing harder.

'Well, who knows what will happen?' he said, the thoughts of the call with Freddie firmly in the back of his mind as he got caught up in the Icelandic magic of the moment.

As if to affirm that, the aurora finally turned up in spectacular style, putting on the most amazing show with its curtains of green and purple that lit up the sky and reflected on the surface of the lake.

'Ah, shame your mum and dad missed this, Rach,' Anna said.

Jonas came up behind his wife and wrapped his arms around her shoulders. 'They were lucky and saw the aurora last time they came. But this is a very good night,' he said, gazing at Rachel with eyes full of love.

The way Jonas looked at Rachel was how Ned felt about Anna. He was starting to realise just how deeply he had fallen for her. If it wasn't for the conversation with Freddie, he could easily find himself getting carried away and maybe carrying out what he'd hinted at to Rachel. He wanted to, he just needed to get this misunderstanding sorted out. Because he was sure that's what it was.

Everyone naturally began to drift off to their cabins once the hot chocolate had run out and the braziers began to lose their heat as the wood burnt down.

Anna hugged her friend.

'It was the perfect wedding, Rach. Just right for you. Even the shoes worked,' she said with a smile.

'Thanks. For everything.'

Ned took Anna's hand and they walked back to their cabin together. It was a little bit cold as the fire that they'd lit earlier had died down but there were enough embers for Ned to be able to coax it back into life while Anna got changed.

From experience, Jonas and Rachel had encouraged their guests to bring thermals to wear in bed. The cabins were really meant for use in the summer months and were cold at this time of year, even with a fire, so although Ned was feeling in a romantic mood after the wedding, the thermals were going to be necessary. Unfortunately.

Anna snuggled under the covers and watched as he undressed, quickly, down to his underwear before pulling on his pyjamas. He turned out the light and got into bed next to her, snuggling against her to get warm. The fire flickered, making the room seem warmer than it was and now that the light was out, the aurora was visible through the window that faced the lake.

Ned spooned her so that they were both facing the window, thinking that this night was going to be pretty hard to beat as romantic nights went. He propped himself up on his elbow so that he could see Anna's face, hoping to say goodnight, maybe more if she'd warmed up, but she was asleep.

Ned smiled, snuggled back down under the layers of sheets and blankets, and slept until morning.

29

The next morning, everyone congregated in the restaurant for breakfast although Rachel and Jonas had already left for their honeymoon. They were going to Canada for a couple of weeks doing hiking or something else that Anna considered far too energetic for a honeymoon. And why you wouldn't go somewhere hot when you lived in Iceland all the time, Anna couldn't understand at all.

The minibuses left for Reykjavik straight after breakfast. Anna and Ned were dropped off last because they lived the furthest into the centre of town. They thanked the driver and wandered up the path to the house. Ned's house. How weird was that?

'I still can't believe this is your house,' Anna said as they unpacked their bags in the mezzanine together.

'I know. Yesterday was so amazing, it's made me even more sure that this is somewhere I want to spend time.'

Anna thought back to when Rachel had first come to Iceland and how quickly she'd fallen for the place, as well as Jonas. At the time, Anna had thought it was all about Jonas, but she was beginning to understand that Iceland had a special appeal to some people and clearly Ned was experiencing the same kind of thing. Anna had grown to love the place, perhaps her feelings towards it were more entwined in her feelings for Ned and Rachel but it wasn't the same affinity that they had.

'I need to talk to you about something,' Ned said, sitting on the edge of the bed, watching her as she finished hanging her clothes up.

He sounded serious, so she put down what she was doing and sat down on the bed beside him.

'So last night, Freddie called me.' Ned was staring at the duvet cover and was tracing his finger around the edge of a flower. 'Why did you leave London, was it something to do with work or with Freddie's wedding?'

Anna caught her breath. She never had told him exactly what happened, leaving him to believe his assumption that she'd been working for the photographer. It hadn't seemed like it mattered, and it would have been embarrassing to explain when they met again in Iceland that she'd lost her job because of what'd happened at the exact moment they'd first met.

'It was to do with that drone that flew over the church.' There was no option but to tell the truth. It was the most important thing because she could sense that there was more to this conversation than Ned wanting to find out her career aspirations.

'Right. How was that anything to do with you?'

'It wasn't. But I was working for the PR company that put together the deal with Hey! magazine for Freddie and Sophia and that drone scuppered the exclusive. I got fired because my boss thought I was the one who leaked the location of the wedding.'

'Right,' he said again, seeming to be carefully assessing everything she said. She felt a little bit like she was on trial.

'That really is it. It wasn't me but I couldn't prove it, so I was the scapegoat. They had to do something to appease the magazine.'

'Right.'

'Christ, Ned! You sound as if you don't believe me, I feel like I'm on the bloody witness stand or something.'

He held his hand up to stop her.

'So, to be clear, you got fired for something that was nothing to do with you.'

'Yes, that's literally the definition of being a scapegoat.'

'But why would they do that if it wasn't you?'

'Because I couldn't prove that it wasn't.'

'You have no idea how it happened?'

'No, it was like the secret of the century. No one knew apart from my boss and his PA and as it wasn't either of them, I was the only one left to accuse.'

'I don't understand.'

'Neither do I.' Anna moved to take his hand, but he stood up almost the instant that she touched him, and he paced across to the other side of the small space.

'Freddie seemed so sure that he'd heard it was you. I don't want to believe it, Anna, but... I don't know what to think.'

'I was going to try and find out who it was, but it was so crap, Ned, losing my job and losing everything that had meant anything to me in London, I just came here instead.'

'But if you'd found out who it was, you could have got your job back and cleared your name.

'I couldn't. Once you're out you're out. No one will touch you. Even if I'd cleared my name, no one would have cared by then and I'd still be nowhere.'

'I don't understand why you didn't try. You're not the kind of person who takes any shit, you haven't taken my shit, yet you walked away from your career over something you didn't do, and you didn't try to fight.'

'Ned, you don't understand.' Anna could feel the frustration building within her and at any moment, hot tears were going to spill from her eyes as she tried to find the words to make him see. 'That job was my whole life. Losing it… it broke me. My whole life was that job. Rachel made me come here because she knew that I needed something to do, away from London. Staying there wasn't going to help. I needed space to think about a new, different kind of life and it's worked because now I know that I'm not going back to a life that is nothing but work. I need more meaning and I have that now.'

Anna stood up and stepped towards Ned, but he backed away, holding his hands up.

'I want to believe you but Fred's my best friend. How can I tell him that I'm with you when he knows what you did?'

'But I didn't, Ned,' she said desperately.

'I know, Anna but there's nothing to prove that. We need to prove it.'

She slumped onto the edge of the bed, sinking her head into her hands. 'It's too late. I wouldn't know where to start. I honestly have no idea what happened, I just know it wasn't me.'

He took a breath and then crouched in front of her, taking her hands in his. The relief that swept over her, realising that he was on her side after all was almost overwhelming. Anna put her arms around his neck and sobbed into his shoulder.

'Thank you for believing me.'

He reached behind his neck and took her hands away, placing them in her lap.

'I'm sorry. I love you, Anna but I have to be sure about this. I want everything with you, but I have to be sure that I'm doing the right thing.'

Anna looked at him in disbelief.

'You don't trust me.'

'I want to trust you, Anna, more than anything.'

'But you're leaving, aren't you?' She said it almost to prove to herself that she was thinking something worse than what was actually about to happen, but she felt the sense of foreboding radiating from Ned before she looked up to see his face full of guilt.

'I'm sorry. I need to sort this out. Before we get in too deep.'

She stood up.

'You do what you need to,' she said, with force, her devastation turning to anger. 'But know this. If you leave now, there is no going back. I understand that you somehow want to make sure I'm not a liar but that says more about you than me.'

Ned visibly cringed.

'Exactly. It's not very nice, is it? Not very nice to feel that you might not know me very well after all. Well, I think I know you. You can't allow yourself to trust anyone, even yourself. What has this been between us, Ned? Because for me, it has been like nothing I've ever had or anything I thought I would have in my life, but I can't carry on with you if you don't trust your judgement about me. I've shown you my whole self and you're throwing it back in my face.'

'Anna— '

'I mean it. Leave now and it's over. This is not the time to take off and mull things over. This is the time to stand by me, believe what I've told you and face the world together. If you want us to work, Ned, that's what you have to do.'

She sniffed and wiped her eyes with her sleeve, looking Ned straight in the eye, daring him to make the wrong decision.

'I… I can't think straight.'

'I'm going to go out for a walk. I'll be an hour. You decide what you want to do and when I get back, you'll either be here or you won't.'

Ned looked at her with desperation in his eyes. She could

see how conflicted he was, and she briefly regretted issuing her ultimatum, but she wasn't the laid-back woman who was enjoying a holiday in Iceland anymore. He'd turned her back into the Anna who lived in London, a person consumed by her job and ruthless with it.

Anna made her way down the ladder while Ned watched, with tears in his eyes. She already knew he wouldn't be there when she got back. She didn't know what it would take for him to see that trusting people, trusting her, was something he was going to have to do if he wanted to move on with his life. She wished she could be the person who helped him to get there but now that he wasn't sure he could trust her, that wasn't to be.

She pulled her coat on and left the house without looking back.   It had been snowing on and off in little flurries since they left the cabin that morning. Breakfast felt like days ago when everything had still been okay. She walked down to the sea and sat on the wall, pulling her hood up and zipping her coat right up. In her haste to leave, she'd forgotten her hat and gloves, but she wasn't thinking that hard about how cold she was. She was wallowing, remembering the day before, how Ned had watched her walk down the aisle, how his eyes had been full of love, and she'd allowed herself to believe that he was hers. And now he wasn't. She thought back to Freddie's wedding and how she'd felt when she'd first met him, that feeling that she now knew was the first tiny spark of attraction between them. And finding him here, in Reykjavik had felt like serendipity. She gave a small laugh through the tears that were falling, thinking that before all of this, before Ned, she would never have believed in stuff like that. She'd almost been scornful of Rachel when she'd fallen for Jonas in such spectacular style but something so similar had happened to her.

When she could take the cold no longer, she stood up,

brushed the snowflakes off her lap and headed towards the nearest coffee shop, the one near Snug, to get something to warm her up before she headed home.

As she ate a pain au chocolate and sipped a steaming latte, she decided this wasn't going to break her. It would be hard to get over Ned, maybe the hardest thing she'd ever have to do but she knew she could do it if she kept busy. Her new business was going to save her and give her a focus when she went back to London. It was time to go back now.

Just before she put the key into the lock when she got back to the house, she took a deep breath and hoped more than anything that now she'd planned on how she'd begin getting over Ned, maybe she wouldn't have to. Maybe he would be sitting on the sofa waiting for her, cleaning his glasses on his shirt with a lopsided smile on his face.

But he wasn't.

Anna gulped down a sob. She'd known this is what would happen and that was hard to take. Harder than she could have imagined but she was going to pick herself up and start her new life. She could do it by herself and the success she would make of it would be all the sweeter for that.

30

Ned couldn't do anything except watch Anna leave the house. Short of telling her to forget he'd ever mentioned the whole business about Freddie's wedding, there was nothing he could say to her to change anything at the moment. He was torn between loyalty to Freddie and the fact that his relationship with Anna was the closest he'd ever come to love.

He climbed down from the mezzanine and headed into the kitchen to find something to drink. He needed to take the edge off while he decided what to do next. Yes, his instinct was to leave but that would mean it was over with Anna and that wasn't what he wanted. He was well and truly outside his comfort zone because up until now, everything complicated in his life had been managed by someone else, hence the reason why the only relationship he'd had for the past ten years was with someone from his publicity team.

The cupboards were empty. He had an hour. He pulled on his coat and hat and headed out to the nearest bar.

Íslenski Barrin was the closest bar, another great reason to have bought the house, thought Ned as he headed up the steps. He went straight to the bar and ordered a double whisky.

'Hey, Ned!'

He turned around to see Brun and Olafur sitting at a table together. All he wanted was a drink and to be alone, but it seemed that wasn't to be.

'Hi, carrying on the celebrations?'

They laughed. '*Skál*!' they said in unison as Ned sat down to join them.

'You are drinking alone?' Brun asked.

Ned exhaled. 'It's been a tough morning.'

'We left you an hour ago,' said Olafur, incredulously. 'What has happened since then?'

Ned explained as briefly as he could the whole thing about Freddie's wedding and Anna's involvement with it.

'But she has said it was not her.' Brun was frowning as he spoke. It was a bit of a wake-up call for Ned. He liked Brun and trusted his straightforward approach to everything.

'Yes, but Freddie said it was.'

'But he has no proof. I do not understand why you would not believe Anna?'

'Fred's my best friend, I have to listen to what he says. Imagine if Anna and I were together and there was all this bad feeling between them, it would be horrible for all of us. I don't want to lose Freddie.'

'But you will lose Anna?' Olafur had been quiet but now asked the most pertinent question.

'I don't know what to do.' Ned pushed his glasses up and rubbed his hands over his face before he downed the rest of his drink.

'If you love Anna, you have to believe her. Why would she lie?' Brun was clearly on Anna's side. He was saying exactly what she had. 'She loves you. All of this happened before you were together. You need to talk to your friend. Or you will lose her.'

'It might already be too late,' said Ned, dejectedly.

'It is never too late.' Olafur banged his hand on the table to prove his point. 'Love is not around every corner, Ned. It is precious and has to be respected.'

Brun raised his eyebrows, looking surprised at his friend's profoundness but he was nodding.

'If you love Anna, you have to fight for the love and that means talking to your friend,' Olafur carried on. 'I think you are not used to this kind of thing. Gudrun says that you have not had a girlfriend before.'

Ned felt himself blush. 'Well, not anyone serious.'

'And not to offend you but I think being a celebrity person is like living in a different world and perhaps that is making it difficult for you and your friend to understand from Anna's perspective.' Olafur added a shrug as if Ned could take his opinion either way.

'Look, man,' said Brun, taking over from his friend, 'you have loved it in Iceland, yes?'

Ned nodded. It was the truth.

'Because of finding your music and finding Anna?'

Ned nodded again.

'Those things together are not a coincidence, Ned. I think you understand.'

Brun was right. Ned saw it with sudden clarity. He'd come here to find his music, but he hadn't hit his stride until he'd met Anna. And then the music had flowed, and the words had meant more. They'd meant everything. Singing that song for her at the open mic night had been one of the highlights of his life and he'd forgotten that. That was the moment when everything had come together for him and somehow, he'd let go of that feeling and now he'd lost her.

'Thank you. You're the best.' Ned stood up and clapped them both on the back before he pulled his coat on. 'I have to go and get my girl.'

31

Anna was wondering if it had been wise to head for the airport without having a flight booked. She went straight to the Icelandair desk and found that she could get a ticket for an evening flight. Still, it felt better to be waiting at the airport rather than waiting in the house. In Ned's house.

She checked in and then headed for the bar which was extortionately expensive but a very nice place to wait for a few hours. She pulled out her laptop and settled in to do some work on setting up some social media posts for her new business.

The open mic night by itself wasn't enough to build a business on, or if it was it would take ages to build into anything she could make a living from. She had decided to target the indie record labels that Ned had suggested to see who was doing the PR for their artists. Her gut feeling was that most small labels wouldn't be able to afford any decent agency so she was hoping to build her business on the promise of great PR for a lower cost than anyone else could offer. She hoped that being able to offer the open mic night as an extra perk would give her a competitive edge. She also knew that most decent PR people that these businesses could afford wouldn't be limiting themselves to operating solely in one area, like emerging music artists, and she thought that by fixing herself into that niche, she could make a name for herself.

Her phone lay on the table next to her laptop and she kept checking it in case there was any word from Ned. But presumably, he was on a plane right now. Maybe that was why she hadn't heard from him or maybe it was because she'd been very clear that she wasn't interested in a relationship with someone who didn't trust her. She realised that she was asking him to choose between his best friend and her. Freddie had been by his side for ten years; they had been through so much together and inhabited a world where they couldn't trust most people, so their bond was more important. She was asking him to choose her over that, based on a few weeks of knowing each other.

Anna had had a couple of coffees but now decided to switch to gin. She ordered a double gin and tonic and then opened her messages and began composing one to Ned. It was important to let him know that she understood and that she knew that it would never work between them because he would never be able to get over the feeling of being unable to trust anyone who hadn't been in that world alongside him.

I'm sorry I made you choose between me and your friend. I understand why you had to choose Freddie. What we had can't exist in the real world. But I did love you, Ned. Anna x

Tears fell down her cheeks as she wrote the message. For such a short message, it took a long time to write but when she'd finished, she was satisfied that it said what it needed to, and she felt like she'd achieved a little bit of closure as she pressed send.

She wiped her tears from her cheeks with the palms of her hands, finding that the barman had brought her another drink. He smiled awkwardly as he set it down.

'I'm sorry you are having a bad day. I hope this helps.'

'Thank you,' said Anna, thinking that his thoughtful gesture summed up the wonderful people that lived in this country perfectly.

He nodded and returned to the bar.

Anna picked up her phone. She had to move on and engaging in messaging to and fro with Ned wasn't going to help anything. Picking herself up and moving on had to be something she did alone. With that in mind, she blocked him just in case he was inclined to respond to her message.

She finished both drinks in quick succession and packed up her things. Having eaten nothing since the pain au chocolate some hours ago, eating something now might be a good idea before the alcohol took too much effect on her empty stomach.

The cafeteria had glass walls which showed that the snow was beginning to settle quite a lot now and from the warmth of the terminal building, Anna was sorry that she hadn't stayed to experience the snow, but it was good that it had held off long enough for Rachel and Jonas to have their perfect wedding.

London after a few weeks felt different. Colder because it was winter now, but it was more than that. It had lost some of the sparkle it had before. Even her flat felt…flat compared to the cosiness of the house in Reykjavik. With fresh eyes, she could see that she had been working in London before, not living in London. She had chosen her flat for its convenience for work, it had been a purely practical decision and she'd never spent enough time there to care what it was like. It was still a convenient place to live, within spitting distance of her open mic night venue and a lot of indie record companies had offices around Soho.

Almost the second she'd woken up on her first day back,

she had an urge to make some changes. She headed out for breakfast and then went shopping for paint and supplies. She spent the whole week repainting the flat, freshening it up with white paint almost everywhere apart from the bedroom which she painted a dark dusty blue. She chose darker accent colours for the paintwork in the lounge and painted the tiny kitchen a strange chartreuse green that she hadn't been able to resist. She cleared out the spare room, arranging for a charity to collect all the furniture in there which had been second-hand in the first place, so that she could turn it into an office.

After all her hard work, Anna treated herself to a trip to Snug's flagship store in Shoreditch and bought more cushions, rugs, throws and lamps than she could carry so she had to splash out on a taxi to get home.

The first thing that she chose a place for was the throw that she'd bought from Snug in Iceland. It went perfectly in her newly decorated lounge, and she'd bought another from the London store that was quite different, but they looked great together. She lay a sheepskin rug on the floor in front of the sofa and arranged some fairy lights and pinecones in the grate of the fireplace that was just for show because the chimney was sealed up. With table lamps on some mismatched side tables next to the sofa, the room was so much better. Fresher, cosier and somewhere that Anna knew she would look forward to spending time in. That was more important now because she was going to be working from home. It had to be somewhere she wanted to be.

Her next makeover project was perfecting her office. That weekend, she headed to Camden market and picked up some vintage records of some of her favourite bands from her teenage years. The bands she liked weren't especially collectable, so she got them for next to nothing and framed them for her office wall. She thought it would be good to remind herself of her love for music since that was what she'd be focusing on now.

All this was a fantastic distraction from thinking about Ned. It wasn't that she hadn't thought about him just that she hadn't allowed herself enough time to dwell on anything. Of course she'd wondered whether Ned had tried to call or message her. There had been a couple of low points when she'd wavered, forgetting that he couldn't be hers, and had hovered her finger over the button to unblock him. But the way he'd made her feel when he'd asked her to prove that she hadn't sabotaged Freddie and Sophia's wedding photoshoot, hadn't left her and it still hurt enough to strengthen her resolve.

The night that she finished her renovations, Anna treated herself to a fancy Pasta Evangelist meal, a chocolate fondant and a bottle of her favourite red wine and sat in her cosy living room with the Gilmore Girls on Netflix. It was all a great distraction but not as good as being physically busy and after a couple of glasses of wine, she couldn't help herself. She picked up her laptop and googled Ned.

The top results were recent posts on his social media feeds but there was also an interview from a couple of days ago with an online music magazine. Anna clicked on it and a photo of Ned filled her screen. It was from a photoshoot, recent by the looks of it because his hair looked the same as it had at the wedding. He looked good and it made her heart ache for him. If she thought there was any possibility of finding out what had actually happened so that she could prove her innocence, she would give it a go. This thought kept flitting around her mind. If she found out, she could get him back. But she didn't know where to start. Everyone she'd thought was a friend was, in hindsight, no more than a colleague and it was still too soon for any of the people at her old agency to speak to her without being guarded about what they were saying.

The interview was about the new direction he was taking since he'd left The Rush and she loved reading his words. It was like sweet torture, hearing them in her head as if he were speaking to her, telling her about his love of finding the words and music to express his emotions. Then her heart almost stopped when she read the next part.

'What's your biggest inspiration?' was the question.

And Ned had responded, 'I spent some time in Iceland, which was amazing. I wrote every day, but nothing came together until I met someone who changed that. She was my inspiration.'

He'd told her that, it was nothing new but the fact he'd said it in an interview. Did that mean something? No, he wasn't saying that he was with her or declaring his undying love but then why mention it at all? If he didn't want her, why hadn't he come up with a stock answer? He must have been trained to be an expert at that when he was in the band.

She scrolled down the page to see if there was anything else he said that would give her an insight into how he was. She missed him so much. Was this what it was going to be like now? Would she be poring over the internet reading about him, watching him live his life at a distance?

'Have you signed a deal with anyone for your solo career?' That was the final question.

'Not yet. I'm still working on a few things, but I went to a couple of open mic nights in Reykjavik which I enjoyed, and I hope to do more of that kind of thing before I settle on how to take it forward.'

Knowing how much he'd loved performing at the open mic nights, Anna was pleased that Ned was going to carry that on. She wanted him to come to her open mic night, although, that would be awful, really awkward. But she did desperately want to see him.

She poured herself another glass of wine. This was a nightmare. Was she ever going to stop thinking about him? It was going to drive her mad. She had never felt like this before, like she needed someone for her basic survival, for her sanity to remain intact. That's what it felt like. It was as if all she was doing to carve out her new life, to start afresh, was a superficial gloss over the fundamental problem; she'd fallen in love with Ned and now he was inextricably part of her life whether she wanted him to be or not. And the problem was, she knew that's exactly what she did want. But in her soul, she knew she couldn't allow herself to be with someone who didn't trust her. Someone who was going to run away at the first sign of anything he thought might be difficult to deal with. Was that any way to live either?

32

With every interview he did, Ned spoke about Anna, not by name, but he knew she'd know it was her if she read it. It was the only way he knew to let her know that he was still in love with her, still thinking about her and lost without her.

When he'd arrived back at the house in Reykjavik after a couple of drinks at the bar with Olafur and Brun, he realised that Anna had left. He was confused, thinking that he had kept track of the time until he pulled his phone out and saw that he had been an hour and a half. After issuing her ultimatum, she must have assumed that he had left while she'd been out.

He'd received her text when he was waiting for a car to take him to Keflavik airport later that evening. It sounded so final. Despite the ultimatum, he'd thought they'd be able to work things out once they had a chance to talk again but when he tried to call, he realised that she'd blocked him. He also realised that he had no other way to contact her once they were back in London. With no job, he couldn't track her down at work, he didn't know where she lived, and he didn't know any of her London friends.

So, for the moment, the interviews were the only way to communicate a tiny bit with her. To let her know that she was

211

his inspiration, that hadn't changed. That he was waiting for her to start the open mic nights so that he could come and support her. He hoped she could read between the lines and know that his feelings hadn't changed. He no longer cared about what had happened at Freddie's wedding, but he did need to square that away with them before he could do anything more to win her back.

Ned had been round to Freddie and Sophia's for dinner when he first got back and had tried to broach the subject of the wedding leak.

'I'm not sure that leak about the wedding was down to Anna after all, having spoken to her,' he said, nonchalantly sipping his wine.

'Ah, right,' said Freddie. 'Did she say what had happened?'

'She didn't know exactly but it wasn't her.'

Sophia tutted. 'I heard it was her from a very reliable source. If she can't tell you who it was, doesn't that kind of say it all?'

'I know her, Sophia, and I trust her. I've lost her over this, and I want to get her back, but I can't…' he coughed, feeling uncomfortable saying what he needed to say in front of Sophia, but she was the ringleader here and the one who needed to hear it. 'I can't lose you, Fred.'

Freddie stood up, took a slug of wine and said, 'Come on Ned, we need to talk. Soph, we'll be upstairs.' He kissed his wife and leaving her looking distinctly pissed off, led the way to his studio.

'Look, I have to stand by Sophia on this. She's my wife, you get that.'

'I know that, man. I told Anna that if she couldn't prove otherwise, we can't go anywhere but I love her, Fred.' Ned walked over to the window, shoved his hands in his pockets and stared out at the slight fog that was settled over London, gently muting the glow from the streetlights.

'Then, work it out with her. This is Sophia's thing, not mine. It's not going to make any difference to our friendship. Yeah, if you're with Anna you guys might not be welcome around here for a cosy dinner but I can work on Soph. You're my best friend. And you look fucking miserable.'

Ned laughed and turned to look at Freddie who had a smile on his face.

'You and me are always going to be okay, Neddy boy. Who said our wives have to be best mates?'

The following day, Ned had another interview, this time on a morning television show in Manchester. He'd taken an early train and was sitting in the green room with a coffee waiting for his slot to come up.

'Hi, Ned.'

He knew who it was and before he even had time to look up to confirm, his heart had sunk. It was Jeannie.

He stood up to greet her with what he hoped was very clearly a platonic peck on the cheek. 'Jeannie, what are you doing here?'

'I'm with Ali today,' she said gesturing to the screen which showed the live feed from the studio where her film star client Ali Fox was busy chatting to the hosts.

'Ah, right.'

'So, how've you been? Still with that woman you met in Iceland?'

He almost asked how she would know about that, but it had been in the press.

'We're not seeing each other at the moment.' That was as close to the truth as he was prepared to go.

'I hear she lost her job over that business at Freddie's wedding when it wasn't even her fault.'

Ned was suddenly more interested in what Jeannie had to say.

'She didn't want to blame it on anyone else.' He just wanted Jeannie to keep talking and didn't want to say anything to make her think that was a bad idea.

Jeannie glanced around the room to make sure that no one was listening and dropped her voice.

'But she knew it was Cassie?'

'Cassie?'

'Cassie Pollard. You know.'

'But she's friends with Sophia.'

'Well, you didn't hear it from me, okay? She's always had a thing for Freddie, and she was jealous as hell that Sophia finally got him to commit. So, if you don't know, I'm guessing Sophia doesn't know either.'

'No, I don't think she does. I'm going to have to tell her, but I'll keep it to myself where I heard it from. Thanks, Jeannie.'

'Anytime.'

'And I really am sorry about the way things were between us. I didn't treat you well, you deserved better than that.'

'I'm just glad you're happy. You look happy.' She squeezed his hand and smiled. 'I have to go and debrief with Ali, and I didn't hear anything she bloody said!'

Ned grinned. He was desperate to get this interview over and done with so that he could get back to London and somehow track Anna down. Maybe he could ask Jeannie where she used to work since she seemed to know so much about everything. They might have a contact number for her. But what if they didn't or what if Jeannie didn't know?

A few minutes later he went on set and was greeted by the hosts, Jake and Kate, while a pre-recorded segment was running. He'd been on the show before with the band, so he knew them both and felt pretty comfortable chatting, especially now he was on a high after the conversation with Jeannie.

'We hear that you've been writing in Reykjavik recently. How's that been? Did you like Iceland?' Jake asked, once they'd talked about leaving the band and what he was planning to do next.

'I loved it, the people are amazing, so friendly. I played an open mic night a couple of times and felt like I discovered my music over there. All thanks to Anna.'

'Anna? Is she someone you're still in touch with?'

That was a delicate way to ask, Ned thought. It didn't put him in an awkward spot by asking outright what their relationship was.

'No, but I'd like to be,' said Ned, smiling. He ought to have been focussing on what was going on in the studio but all he could think about was Anna. If she was watching, maybe she'd get in touch.

'Great to hear what you've been up to. Thanks for coming in, Ned,' Kate said, wrapping things up.

'Thanks for having me, guys.'

As soon as he was back in London, he called Freddie and arranged to meet him in a pub near his house. The locals that drank in there were used to them and never batted an eyelid, treating them the same as anyone else. They ordered a pint of the guest ale each and chose a table in a quiet corner.

'I saw Jeannie this morning and found out from her that it definitely wasn't Anna that leaked about the wedding.'

'That's good news,' Freddie said, heaving a sigh of relief. 'Honestly, I'm fed up with hearing about it. Who was it then?'

'Cassie somebody.'

'Christ. I always thought there was something weird about her. Soph's going to be pissed off that it was one of her friends, though.'

'Sorry to say it but that's your problem,' Ned said with a smug smile. He was glad to see Freddie squirm a little given how he'd just landed the whole thing with Anna at Ned's door expecting him to somehow deal with it. He'd lost Anna because he was trying to please his friend. It was clear to him now that it never should have come to that and that he should never have asked Anna to prove herself to him. No wonder she'd blocked him and ended things. It was what he deserved, Brun and Olafur had been right.

'Nice to see you happy again, Ned. I assume you're back together then?'

'No, I asked her to prove herself and she's cut me out of her life, and I can't blame her. It was a horrible way for me to treat her after all we'd had in Iceland. Nothing's the same without her beside me. I have to get her back.'

'I feel partly responsible. I didn't realise things were that serious between you.'

Ned shrugged. 'I didn't realise it myself until she was gone. We've spent so long in our tiny circle of trusted people that we automatically assume anyone outside of that is out to get us. In Iceland, things were easier, and I didn't think like that, but then the couple of times when real life broke through, I panicked and forgot that Anna was on my side. I put the barriers up and shut her out as if she was part of the problem.'

'Have you tried talking to her?'

'I don't know where she lives, and she's blocked me.'

'Mate, it's the twenty-first century. You don't need to know her name and address so you can look her up in the telephone directory. Can't you DM her?'

Ned shook his head. It had crossed his mind. It would be so easy. Even if he didn't go as far as to DM her, he could put a supportive comment on one of her Twitter posts. Something like that could start a conversation. But it wasn't fair to her and once he explained it to Freddie, he understood. Anna was trying to get her business off the ground on her own merit and showing up in her Twitter feed could take that away from her. It was impossible to stay under the radar even with a pseudonym and unless he used his own account, how would she know it was him anyway?

'When I was on the TV this morning, I kind of shouted her out and said I wanted to get in touch. I doubt she saw it, but it seemed worth a try.'

'What's plan B, just in case she wasn't watching for that half a minute today?'

Ned outlined his tentative idea. 'We owe her, Fred. If it wasn't for that friend of Sophia's, Anna wouldn't have lost her job.'

They came up with a plan of action. It might have involved playing the long game for much longer than Ned would have liked, but it was a solid plan and Ned was confident that it would show Anna how much she meant to him and hoped that it would win her over.

33

Anna had booked dates for the open mic night to run once a week in the run-up to Christmas. There were only going to be three, given that it was the end of November already, but she thought it was good timing with the pubs busier than ever, it might build some momentum which she could pick up on in the new year, rather than starting from scratch in January when everyone was down in the dumps.

She had chosen a pub in Soho which wasn't one of the typically trendy ones. Those were always too busy anyway. The one she'd picked, The Glover's Needle, was kind of old-fashioned with room for the event to spread out from the corner that she'd agreed into more of the space if it went well. She'd negotiated the space for free on the promise that she would take care of the advertising and present a full list of acts. It was a tall order for the first one because she couldn't rely on people just rocking up and being willing to play on the first night when no one knew about it. No, she had to get some pre-booked acts in to bolster it and then fill the gaps with people who turned up on the night.

The couple of record companies she'd emailed that Ned had suggested hadn't responded but now that she had definite dates, she followed up with a phone call to each of them.

The first one she called was not interested at all, even when she decided to mention that she was a friend of Ned Nokes, but Soho Record Company remembered her email and apologised for not replying. They were launching a new band in March the following year and were looking for a venue to help them begin to get a feel for performing acoustically somewhere out of their comfort zone. It seemed perfect. They offered to advertise the open mic night on their website and said that the band would spread the word to their fans to help with audience numbers.

Anna was thrilled. It was more than she could have hoped for. If she pulled it off, she might be able to collaborate with the label to help with marketing and PR for this band's launch and get paid for it.

But one band wasn't going to fill her list for the first night so she began trawling through Instagram and Twitter looking for local acts that she might be able to tempt into signing up. It was easier than she thought. Musicians wanted nothing more than to play, it turned out. She came up with a standard package of social media pushes that she offered to them in return. In the week leading up to the open mic night, she would be posting about them individually and then the day after she would share photos and clips of the performances. It was all things that they could have done themselves but probably wouldn't, and she hoped that once she gained traction, she would have a better reach than any of them individually anyway.

By the time the first date arrived, Anna had filled seven of the fifteen ten-minute spots. In an ideal world, she would have preferred to have been on ten, with five to fill on the night but she'd agreed with the record label that their band could go last and fill any extra time with a longer set.

There was an hour to kill before she needed to leave the

flat and she didn't know what to do with herself. It had been an odd day. She was super excited, but it was sad at the same time. She'd had this idea in Iceland and shared it with Ned and now that it was happening, she wanted him to be by her side to see it.

Since the night when she'd googled him and read the interview with the music magazine, she had stayed away from looking at anything to do with him. It was too hard. Being busy again had helped but she didn't miss him any less than she had when she'd left Iceland.

She was aimlessly scrolling through her Twitter feed when her phone buzzed with a FaceTime call from Rachel.

'Hey, Mrs Einarsson, how was the honeymoon?' Anna had been desperate to speak to Rachel but hadn't wanted to intrude. She was thrilled to bits to hear from her friend.

'It was amazing! We did cross country skiing through the most amazing forests; it was all log fires and amazing food, and everything was beautiful. And very romantic.'

'Glad to hear it. That's what you want from a honeymoon.'

'So how are things with you and Ned?'

'Things with me are great. It's my first open mic night tonight at The Glover's Needle and I'm shitting myself.'

'That's brilliant! I can't believe you've got that off the ground already.'

'It's been a good distraction. Me and Ned, well, we're not me and Ned anymore.'

Anna explained everything to her friend who was as expected, totally on her side.

'He's an idiot, Anna. I mean, who keeps running off like that the minute things get a bit uncomfortable or tricky? It's crazy. I guess celebrities are a different breed.'

'That's what I decided in the end.'

'But he did say that nice thing on the TV the other day.'

'What?'

'I saw that clip of him on the BBC morning show the other day. He said that you were his inspiration and that he'd lost touch but wished he hadn't.'

'Really?'

'Go and watch it. You might understand what he means. I'd just assumed you were still together, and he was being cagey to protect you.' Rachel paused and then said, 'Do you still love him, after all of that?'

Anna sighed. 'I tried not to, but I do. I feel like there's a part of me missing. I've tried to move on, you know, been busy building my business but there's still a hole where Ned fits and I don't know if it'll ever go away.'

'It will. It's because he's the first person who you've really been in love with. It's hard to get over something like that but you will.'

'But what if there's no one else that loves me like that, Rach?'

Rachel was the only person that Anna could share her biggest fear with. What if there was never anyone who loved her, who she loved as much as Ned?

They chatted for a while longer and then Anna had to hang up because it was time for her to go.

When she arrived at The Glover's Needle, she sat at the end of the bar chatting with the barman, Joe, between him serving customers. Two people turned up to put their names down which wasn't bad for the first week.

Once the first act started and received a supportive reception from the small crowd that were probably ninety per cent fans of the band the record label had sent, Anna began to relax and enjoy the music, making sure that she remembered to take pictures and make notes about each of the acts for her social media posts the following day. The band came on at the end and did a thirty-minute set which went down well. They were called Tuft and reminded her of the indie bands of the nineties in the best way. By the time they'd finished, most of the customers in the pub were listening, even if they hadn't been to begin with, and the crowd around Anna's corner of the pub had grown considerably. She felt sure she could claim that the night had been a success. All the acts signed up to play the following week and a couple of people in the crowd put their names down too.

Anna got home late but elated and fell into bed exhausted but happier than she'd felt for a few weeks.

The next day she worked hard on posting on social media, to keep her promise to the acts that had supported her and by the time she looked at the clock, it was lunchtime. Needing some fresh air, she left the flat and headed to her favourite deli to grab something to eat along with a coffee. It was so cold out, that she wished she'd remembered to put a hat on.

When she left the shop with a toasted cheese focaccia and a latte, heading back to the flat, she bumped into someone who was wandering along, looking at their phone rather than where they were going. When he looked up in surprise that he'd walked into someone, she realised it was Freddie Banks.

'Oh, I'm so sorry,' he said with a smile that made Anna realise how he had managed to become a heartthrob.

'No problem,' she said, smiling back.

He looked at her, still smiling but with a slight frown of confusion. 'Have we met?'

'No,' she said truthfully.

'Oh, okay. Well, sorry again.'

Anna gave a small nod and walked around him.

'Hey,' she heard him call. 'Are you Anna?'

How could he possibly have realised that? They'd never met. Apart from when she'd addressed the congregation at his wedding. Apart from that.

She turned around. 'Yes. Hi.'

He smiled a little awkwardly. 'Ned misses you, you know.'

Does he? 'Oh.'

'He knows it wasn't you, the leak.'

'Oh, right.'

'Honestly. It was a friend of my wife's.'

He looked sheepish which told Anna that he was telling the truth and that it was taking a lot for him to admit it to her.

'Ned's been trying to get in touch.'

Anna's heart began to race. He wanted to talk to her.

'Okay, thanks.' What else could she say?

She turned and carried on walking, hearing Freddie say, 'Oh, right.'

There was nothing to be gained from talking to Freddie anymore. Yes, she could have said she missed Ned and known that he would relay that back. It would have been the easiest thing in the world to give her number to Freddie to pass on. But as much as she missed and loved Ned, she had to know that he understood that it was not okay to run away at the first sign of trouble like he had done before. Twice.

Ned was going to have to prove himself. Let him miss her. Let Freddie go back and tell him that he'd seen her and see what he did with that. Let him have to track her down and stand outside the deli every day until the next time she decided to call in for a lunchtime sandwich. Ned had made everything harder than it needed to be with his trust issues and unawareness of how the real world could treat someone, even if they'd done nothing wrong. As a person who inhabited the real world, she needed someone who was going to be on her side in that world, not someone who had existed for far too long in a bubble which was almost entirely cut off from reality. She deserved someone who would fight for her, take her at her word, love her and know her regardless of what anyone else might say.

Anna wanted Ned to be that man, but he was going to have to show her that he could be.

When she got home, she turned on the TV and ate her lunch in a bit of a daze. Would Freddie be telling Ned now that he'd seen her?

Once she'd finished eating, she went into her office and ignoring the little voice that was telling her it was becoming an obsession, googled Ned again to see if the clip of him on the BBC morning show that Rachel had been talking about was there. It was. She pressed play.

After fast-forwarding through most of the programme, Anna watched the segment with Ned at the end. He looked completely different to the last time she'd seen him. Happy, which was great, but more than that, he seemed… jubilant. The only time she'd ever seen him like that before was when he'd played at the open mic night.

When she watched him say that he wanted to be in touch again, she felt like he was asking her. For him to be so happy, sure enough of himself to say something in public, he must've known then that she wasn't the leak.

It was so confusing. On the one hand, she missed him so badly that it didn't seem like anything should be an obstacle to them getting back together, especially when she saw him there, wanting her, being so smiley and happy. She wanted to be with him, sharing that joy.

But if he hadn't found out that the leak was down to someone else, what would be happening then? Would he still want her, or would they forever be pining away for each other because he couldn't take her word for something? Something that seemed so much less important and earth-shattering than it had a few months ago. Because now she had found her way through when she'd thought all was lost. She'd found herself and her life was more meaningful because of what had happened at the church that day, so it was hard not to look back and think that whoever had leaked the location of the wedding had done her a favour.

34

It had been the worst possible day. Anna had woken up to find her flat was freezing cold because her heating hadn't come on and after some investigative googling, it turned out that it wasn't working at all. No heating, no hot water and to top it all it had started snowing.

It was the day of her last open mic night before Christmas and she had gained so much momentum from the last two weeks that she had been super confident about having a full list of acts without having to hand over a whole bunch of slots at the end to her back-up act from the record company. Not that Tuft weren't brilliant, and grateful for her interest in them, but when she had given them one less slot last week than they'd had the week before, it had felt like a win.

Aside from that, it had been a tough week. Since she'd seen Freddie over a week ago outside the deli, there had been nothing from Ned. She had felt sure that it would be easy enough for him to track her down on Twitter or something, especially since he knew the record company that was helping her out. He'd put a word in for her for goodness' sake, so the only explanation could be that he had changed his mind. Perhaps Freddie had told him that she hadn't seemed interested, but she'd been so sure after seeing him on television that he was going to actively try to find her that she'd taken that thought and run with it.

Whatever it was that had kept him away, made him change his mind, Anna didn't know. Her mood had sunk lower and lower as each day with no contact from him rolled around and she began to dwell on all the reasons why he wouldn't want her and there were plenty of those that she could torture herself with. She'd gone from having love-hearts for eyes, telling herself not to throw herself into his arms the moment she finally saw him again to realising that she was kidding herself. He wasn't coming for her, so she was back to trying to forget that she'd ever thought that Ned was falling in love with her, and it was harder than ever.

The last thing she could face was her open mic night finale being ruined by snow and then with that disappointment over, to return to a freezing cold flat after she'd traipsed home through what looked likely to be several inches of snow by then. With no hope of tracking down a reliable plumber in the space of an afternoon, she decided to give herself a break and booked a room at the nearby Travelodge. Being self-employed meant she had to watch the pennies but although it was fairly cheap, especially for Covent Garden, it was going to be warm with hot water and that's all she needed.

Before she left for The Glover's Needle, she packed an overnight bag, said a quick prayer to the plumbing gods that her pipes wouldn't burst while she was out and headed down the stairs.

The snow was still falling which was fairly unusual for London and Anna felt sure that by tomorrow it would all be grey slush. Although she was annoyed with its timing, she did take a few moments to appreciate how lovely it was as it crunched beneath her feet. Being in Iceland once it got really cold had prepared her well. She was wearing her scratchy hat that Rachel had knitted and woolly gloves along with the big coat that Rachel had lent her, insisting that she keep it for all the return visits to Reykjavik she would make.

Anna smiled and pulled out her phone to call Rachel from the snow. 'Look!' she said, holding the phone up high and twirling round with it so that Rachel could see.

'You've got as much snow as us! I can't believe it! That never happened when I lived in London.'

'I'm trying to look on the bright side because it's going to ruin my last open mic night. And my heating's broken.'

'You can't blame the snow for that.'

'I suppose not.'

Rachel was curled up in the corner of her sofa, the soft light from her many table lamps making it look cosier than Anna remembered. She suddenly felt a pang of homesickness for the place. She knew being homesick was usually to do with people rather than an actual place, but she missed Rachel and she missed the only place on earth that she'd ever been in love with anyone. She missed the hope that had given her, the joy and happiness that she was terrified of never having again.

'Anna…'

She hadn't even heard the last thing that Rachel had said, and her friend was looking at her with concern.

'I need to go, Rach. I'll call you tomorrow. Bye.'

She ended the call before Rachel could object and put her phone in her pocket.

Swallowing a sob, she turned her face up to the sky, letting the cold snowflakes fall on her face. Somehow it helped and after a few seconds she wiped her gloved hand across her cheeks and carried on to the pub.

Joe was cleaning glasses, so she took her usual seat at the end of the bar and pulled out her notepad just in case anyone turned up wanting a slot, although by the looks of things it seemed unlikely.

'Been a bit quiet today,' said Joe. 'We had a couple of calls to see if you were still running tonight but I expect the snow will put people off.'

Anna managed a tight-lipped smile, annoyed that Joe had voiced her worst fear. Hopefully, as long as Tuft turned up, which she felt sure they would, it'd be okay.

'And there's a bloke over there who came in looking for you.' Joe nodded towards the opposite side of the room which was obscured from Anna's view by a wood and stained-glass panel.

She stumbled as she got off the stool, wishing that she had checked her make-up when she'd arrived. She probably had mascara all over her face after getting snowy. All she could think was that it could be Ned. That thought was so strong that it stopped her from taking a minute to go to the Ladies and check and instead she just ran her index fingers underneath her eyes and hoped for the best.

Her heart was beating so hard that she could barely see straight but then it stopped. Because it wasn't Ned. A wave of devastation engulfed her, so strong that she had to steady herself by gripping the edge of a table. She was a fool. It was never going to be Ned.

'Giles, how are you?'

Her old boss leapt up, flustered, because he still thought it was good manners to stand if a lady approached a table to sit down and hadn't seen her coming. It gave her a few seconds to gather herself. She sat down on the banquette opposite him and consciously told herself not to take any crap. Whatever he was here for, she had to show him that he hadn't broken her and that she was still the strong, determined, capable woman he had fired. It was the worst day for her to need to be all of those things, but she wasn't going to give him the satisfaction of thinking that she was no longer the ruthless PR executive that he remembered.

'Anna, I'm very well. Can I get you a drink?'

'No, thank you. Joe said you were asking for me?'

Perhaps Giles had forgotten that she always liked to get straight to the point and the fact that he had fired her made small talk improbable.

He sat down. 'I hear on the grapevine that the source of the leak that led to that unfortunate business with the drone has been identified.'

'So I believe.' There was no way that she would make whatever he was here for easy.

'In which case, I owe you an apology.'

'Thank you.' She couldn't help being taken aback. He'd been wrong to fire her, but it was unprecedented for someone in his position to seek out the wronged person so long after the event. Normally it was all brushed under the carpet and never mentioned again, no matter what might come to light later on.

'I hope you haven't come here to offer me my job back.'

It was a risky and bold thing to say but Giles's face told Anna that she'd hit the nail on the head. If she'd wanted her job back, she might have played it differently, but she was past that now.   'It's impressive what you've started to do here.'

'Thank you but it's hardly that. Three open mic nights and a few Twitter posts aren't setting the world on fire.'

Taking her cue to explain himself, Giles breathed in heavily before he spoke.

'I understand that you have a... relationship with someone who we are very keen to acquire as a client.'

'Ah, I see. So, I can have my job back if I bring you Ned Nokes.'

'It's a good offer, Anna. You know we're the best and surely you would want that for your...'

Giles floundered for the word as if he couldn't bring

himself to believe that Ned might be in a relationship with her.

'I'm sorry you've wasted your time but I'm not in a relationship with Ned Nokes. If I was, I'd be advising him to steer clear of any agency that treats its loyal staff as badly as you treated me.'

'Anna…'

'Giles. If it wasn't for the fact you think I can bring you Ned Nokes, you wouldn't be here, and you'd never have apologised to me for what you did. I don't expect you've given me a second thought until you realised that I might be useful to you after all and that you'd better come grovelling. And you know what? You should want Ned. He's going to go stratospheric with his solo stuff and if I ever see him again, I'll be sure to tell him exactly where not to go for his PR.'

She stood up, enjoying watching Giles try and fail to come up with something to say.

'If you want to sign up to play, I'll be at the end of the bar.'

Going back to her stool at the end of the bar with a grin on her face, she ordered a gin and tonic from Joe and checked her Twitter feed where she saw a tweet from Tuft to their followers giving the open mic night a shout-out. Things were beginning to look up.

The mood was very festive and although not all of the slots were filled, a couple of young women who hadn't signed up but were watching came up to Anna in the interval and asked if they could play some festive songs. It was the best decision Anna could have made. All thoughts of carefully curating the music went out of the window in the face of a crowd of music lovers who just wanted to celebrate the fact that it was only a few days until Christmas. The one woman borrowed a guitar from someone, and she played while her friend, who had the most beautiful voice, sang the songs. They were melodic, heartfelt versions of classics like, I Wish it Could be

Christmas Every Day and everyone was waving their arms in the air and had the lights on their phones which boosted the atmosphere before Tuft came on to finish the night. They did a couple of their own songs and then asked the two women up to join them in playing more Christmas songs. Anna couldn't have planned the night better if she'd tried. It was memorable enough to be fresh in everyone's minds until well into the new year and if anything was going to help spread the word, it was this.

By the end of the evening, everyone in The Glover's Needle were best friends, bonded over an exceptional night. One of those special things that just happens but when it does, no one forgets. Anna made a start on some social media while Tuft packed up their gear and Joe cleaned up the bar.

'Hey, Anna, want to join us for a drink?' asked Drew, their lead singer and unofficial head of the band.

She was tired but still euphoric and the thought of going back to the Travelodge alone which would immediately depress her was not appealing. Drew had overheard her telling Joe about her heating woes, so it was probably a pity invite but that was fine.

Once they were ready to leave, Anna wished Joe a Merry Christmas and gave him a peck on the cheek, making him blush, then made her way outside with the guys. The snow had stopped but London hadn't managed to spoil its beauty yet. It was still untrodden in many places, only the tyre tracks on the roads marring its perfect whiteness. The way it absorbed the sound, making everything quiet and muffled was something that always took Anna back to her childhood, remembering those amazing days when the snow would be a surprise and the whole family would go sledging, even her mum.

'Are you a snow fan or not?' Drew asked her as they made their way to wherever it was they were going.

'I am tonight. I thought it'd make the night a total wash out, but it was brilliant. Your set was amazing. Inviting those women up to play with you was a stroke of genius.'

He grinned. 'Thanks. We hadn't played live much before your open mic nights. We used to spend all our time practising. I don't know what we were thinking. You're never going to make it if you don't put yourself out there, right?'

'Right. I have a friend who is starting out and he did the same. I think it helps you to know that you're on the right track. It's scary but great, at least it was for him.'

'Has he played here?'

'No, but he did kind of give me the idea.'

'You're onto a winner. The social media stuff you do has got us a load more followers and the record company are on about putting on a proper gig for us in the new year.'

'That's brilliant! Congratulations.'

Drew shrugged and grinned. 'Team effort I reckon. I think Soho Records are going to call you about helping them out with the PR'

For a day that had started so badly, it was shaping up to be one of the best. Here was the first tiny spark that was the start of her business. This was what she had hoped would happen and even though it hadn't happened yet, there was definite reason to be hopeful.

'Where are we heading?'

'I don't know, Will knows the way,' he said, nodding his head towards his bandmate who was walking ahead of them.

As they approached Seven Dials, Anna began to hear music. She wasn't sure where it was coming from. Not from a pub or club because it wasn't loud, thumping bass, it was someone singing and playing the guitar. They emerged from Monmouth Street onto the snow-covered cobbles of Seven Dials where a man was standing in the middle, at the foot of the monument.

Anna recognised the song before she recognised the man.

It was Ned.

He was wearing his usual outfit of dark jeans and black boots with the huge puffer coat he'd worn in Iceland. The black beanie hat was pulled well down over his forehead but the glasses that he'd worn the whole time she'd known him had gone. Anyone watching and paying attention to his voice would know it was Ned Nokes.

It was the song he had written about her, the first one he had played her in his apartment in Reykjavik.

She stopped, the Tuft guys stopping too. Drew was smiling at her in a knowing way that made Anna realise that this was no coincidence.

'Think you're okay from here?' he asked.

Was she?

'Yes, I don't know what's going on but thanks for tonight.'

'Merry Christmas, Anna.'

Anna stood, listening to Ned play, the fairy lights that were strung from the top of the monument and splayed out to the buildings surrounding it were twinkling gently, reminding her of Reykjavik, even if she hadn't already been transported back there by Ned.

She wasn't sure that he'd noticed her. He had his eyes closed as he sang, his emotions there in his voice and in the beautiful words he had written. About her.

He got to the end of the song before he opened his eyes and his gaze settled on her. But she stayed where she was. She'd been determined all along not to throw herself back into his arms, so as hard as it was, she forced herself to stay where she was. It was up to Ned.

To her surprise, he began playing again when she was half-expecting him to have come over to her. It wasn't a song that she recognised but it made her heart soar as the most perfect combination of notes came from his guitar, somehow managing to embody all the feelings that were surging inside her into a melody. As tears began to well in her eyes, Ned began to sing.

My heart is yours,
While we're under the stars.
The words were for her.
I broke your heart,
Let me mend it.
Our destiny is to be entwined,
For however long is forever.

They were an apology and a promise for the future, all at once.

A few people had paused their journey across Seven Dials to listen to this man, busking in the snow in the most unlikely of places. Anna was once again, overwhelmed by a feeling of devastation that the song and this magical moment was going to end but was at the same time wishing it away so that she could go to him.   She didn't care who saw and she was guessing that by virtue of the location he'd chosen and the fact that he was singing an apology song to her in public, Ned didn't either.

He played the final few notes and stood for a few seconds before he began playing again. But Anna could wait no longer. She crossed the road onto the island in the middle where Ned was, and his face broke into a huge smile. He swung his guitar around his body onto his back and came towards her.

'You came. I thought it was you, but my glasses kept misting up in the snow, so I had to take them off. You heard it though?'

Anna nodded. 'It was beautiful.'

'All I want is you, Anna. I've been a total idiot.'

A few more people had gathered around, watching to see what was happening in the middle of the road junction.

'You can't run away from me, Ned. If we're going to be together, we have to have each other's backs. It has to be us against the world, no matter what.'

'I know that and I'm sorry. Not being with you these last few weeks has made me realise what I'd lost. It sounds like an excuse, but I haven't been used to thinking about anyone else except myself. I can't promise I can change overnight but know that I want you to call me out on it when it happens.'

Anna thought back to the last time they'd been together in the bedroom at the house in Reykjavik when she'd told Ned that he needed to have her back.

He could tell what she was thinking because he tilted his head to the side and gave a resigned nod. 'I know you tried before and I wouldn't listen, but I understand now, believe me.'

'I do believe you.' Anna took his freezing hands in hers. 'I feel the same way.'

'So… we're back together?'

'We are.'

Anna threw her arms around his neck, and he picked her up and twirled her around to claps and cheers from the much bigger crowd of people gathered around, some of them filming on their phones.

'I think everyone's going to know now,' Ned said, raising a hand to acknowledge the cheers in true popstar style.

'I don't care, I want everyone to know.'

'Me too.'

35

Anna was busy packing bottles of sloe gin and wine into a rucksack.

'Have you got the books?' called Ned from the lounge.

'Yes, I've got everything. All you need to remember is your guitar. And contact lenses because it's snowing.'

Ned came into the kitchen without his glasses on, so he'd presumably thought about that already.

'It seems a shame to head out into the snow when it's so cosy here,' he said, wrapping his arms around Anna's waist.

She kissed him and then gently removed his hands.

'I totally agree but we can't be late. It's a very important evening for Rachel. It's her first Christmas here and *Jolabokaflód* is a big deal.'

'So, we're going to have to spend the whole evening reading?'

'No, of course not. We'll all exchange books though, but we'll just chat, and you can play some Christmas songs or something. Rachel wants to make it a mash-up of Icelandic and English traditions.'

'Okay. But do we have plenty of wine?'

Anna gave him a gentle shove. 'Yes. It'll be fun.'

They both took a few minutes to get all their outdoor gear

on. Although it had only been a few weeks since they'd been away from Iceland, the weather had turned distinctly wintery in the meantime, and it was snowing almost all the time. But the house was so cosy that it didn't feel remotely bleak. Ned had insisted on a huge shopping spree as soon as they'd arrived so that they could make the place their own. Now it was full of throws, different furniture, lamps and rugs and the cupboard in the kitchen was full of cold weather gear for each of them.

'Ready?'

They left the house and walked down the cobbled path to the street where considering it was early evening on Christmas Eve and verging on a snowstorm, there were a surprising number of people out and about. The atmosphere was festive, and people were huddled in groups against the snow, laughing and chatting as they hurried to wherever they were going.

'Isn't it amazing?' Anna said, beaming at Ned as she got caught up in the mood on the street.

He nodded and took her hand in his, squeezing it. 'I feel really lucky to have this place.'

They arrived at Jonas and Rachel's before the others which Anna was pleased about because she hadn't managed to catch up properly with Rachel since she'd been back. Gudrun and Olafur were having a family dinner and were coming along afterwards, and Brun and Kristin were following as soon as Brun had closed up the office for the Christmas break.

Jonas led Ned into the kitchen with the promise of some special beer that he wanted Ned to try. Anna was sure that it had been carefully engineered by Rachel so that she could quiz Anna on exactly how she and Ned were back together.

'It turned out that he'd been planning it for a couple of weeks and had the guys from Tuft in on it to make sure I went to Seven Dials after the open mic night.'

Rachel topped up their wine from the bottle that Jonas had bought in and put on the coffee table.

'Have you talked about what went wrong?'

'About the fact he didn't stick up for me?'

Rachel nodded. 'I'm surprised you could get over that. I'm not sure you would have a few months ago.'

'Things are different now. I'm different and I know that I love him. I could have walked away, I mean, I did try to, but I was honestly lost without him. Not in the sense that I couldn't carry on without him because I did, but I just knew that part of me would always be missing. That was how much he meant to me, and it sounds crazy but when he sang that song on the traffic island, in the snow, it made me realise that he was lost without me too.'

'Oh my god, Anna. See? This is what love is. You thought I was bonkers when I moved here to be with Jonas, but you understand now.'

Anna nodded, a big smile on her face. 'I do. And I know there will still be things that might trip us up along the way, but I feel so sure that we're in this together now, for good.'

'Well, isn't that the best Christmas present ever?' Rachel said, taking a swig of her wine before she got up to answer the door.

'*Gleðileg jól!*' Gudrun sang from the hallway as she and Olafur pulled off their boots and coats before they came inside.

'Merry Christmas!' Jonas replied, emerging from the kitchen with Ned following behind carrying a couple more wine glasses.

'Shall we wait for Brun and Kristin before we do gifts?' Anna asked.

'Yes, they won't be long,' Rachel said. 'In the meantime, I have something to show you.'

She reached down the side of the sofa and pulled out a

copy of Hey! magazine. Flicking the pages quickly and expertly until she saw what she was looking for, Rachel held it up for all of them to see. It was a full-page photograph of Ned and Anna kissing next to the Seven Dials monument. It was exactly as Anna remembered it in her head although it was strange seeing it from another perspective. The photographer had perfectly captured the moment as if it were the ending of a romantic movie with the snowflakes gently falling and the fairy lights overhead giving the whole picture a Christmassy glow.

'Oh, wow, that is beautiful,' said Gudrun with a dreamy look on her face. 'So romantic. Did you play your guitar in the snow?'

'It's not my best one but yes, I did.'

'What did you play?' Jonas asked.

'One that you've heard before.'

'And a new one,' said Anna. 'But he'll never play that again.'

Ned looked at her, his eyes sparkling and smiling at her.

'Can I keep that?' she asked Rachel.

Rachel hesitated just long enough for Anna to know that she didn't want to part with it and laughed at her friend.

'It's okay, I can take a picture of it to have on my phone.'

Brun and Kristin arrived, and everyone exchanged their gifts, all books in keeping with the Icelandic tradition of Christmas Eve.

'This is great, thanks,' Ned said to Brun as he flicked through his book which was a copy of The Birth of Loud, about the rivalry between two of the biggest guitar makers of all time. 'I might want to read all night after all.'

'No way, we're having a sing-along, right?' said Brun.

Ned nodded to his guitar which was propped up in the corner of the lounge. 'It's all yours, man.'

Brun laughed, but he took Ned up on the offer, everyone

cheering him along.

'Thank you, thank you,' he said, strumming an opening chord. He began to play Silent Night, singing the words in Icelandic. The repetition meant that it was fairly easy for Anna, Ned and Rachel to join in at least the first few words of each line of each verse.

'Play something traditional for an Icelandic Christmas,' said Ned, once Brun had played the final chord and everyone had finished clapping.

'There is a song about the Yule lads.'

'What are the Yule lads?' Ned asked.

'Every night for thirteen nights before Christmas, a Yule lad visits a child's home and brings sweets or something not as nice if the child has been naughty. You put a shoe in the window and the Yule lads leave the gift in the shoe,' Jonas explained.

'Yes, the Yule lads!' chanted Gudrun and Kristin, laughing at each other.

Later that night, tucked into their cosy bed in the mezzanine with candles flickering, making shadows that danced across the ceiling, Ned pulled Anna closer to him.

'This place feels more like home than anywhere else.'

'Mmm. I know what you mean. I feel like this is home for us, we've never been together anywhere else.'

'Apart from the night you stayed over at mine in London,' said Ned.

'That was literally because I had no heating,' Anna teased.

'Not because I serenaded you in the snow?'

'I loved seeing that photo of us. Is that weird? I feel like we ought to be affronted that our privacy was invaded or something.'

'I wasn't trying to be private, Anna. I wanted to tell the world that I was sorry and that I love you. I don't think I've ever been happier to see a photo of myself in the press.'

'Really? You don't mind?'

'No. This is us. Me and you together, there's nothing to hide.'

Note from the Author

In many of the reviews for Snug in Iceland, readers had wondered whether there would be a sequel. I'd never intended to write one but it did make me wonder whether there could be another Icelandic story to tell. Once I'd decided to write it, I loved going back to visit Rachel, Jonas and Reykjavik and hope that you enjoyed finding out what happened to Rachel through Anna and Ned's story.

Thank you to everyone who took the time to leave a rating on Amazon for Snug in Iceland. It really does mean the world to me and this book wouldn't have been written without you.

My local independent bookshop, The Malvern Book Cooperative, have been hugely supportive and I am very proud to be stocked there - the only bricks and mortar shop that I am in. I think they have been as surprised as me how many copies of Snug they have sold!

Thanks to Alison May and Janet Gover for their fantastic weekend writing workshop earlier this year which set me on the way with this book. Janet forced me to rewrite the plot before I was allowed down to the bar one evening - very savvy tactics!

Thank you to my amazing friend Catrin for proofreading and editing for me again and to Alison Milton for proofreading and reassuring me that it wasn't rubbish. My cover designer, Berni Stevens, has done a fantastic job yet again, making sure that Snug and Hideaway look like they belong together. Thanks Catherine for helping me on the last-minute title dilemma, I think it's perfect!

And lastly, thank you James for being the first person to read this book and for loving it.